THE GHOST OF
GRAYLOCK

DAN POBLOCKI

SCHOLASTIC INC.

No part of this publication may be reproduced, stored in a retrieval system, or transmitted in any form or by any means, electronic, mechanical, photocopying, recording, or otherwise, without written permission of the publisher. For information regarding permission, write to Scholastic Inc., Attention: Permissions Department, 557 Broadway, New York, NY 10012.

This book was originally published in hardcover by Scholastic Press in 2012.

ISBN 978-0-545-40269-9

12 11 10 9 8 7 6 5 4 3 2   14 15 16 17 18 19/0

Printed in the U.S.A. 40

This edition first printing, July 2014

The text type was set in Adobe Caslon Pro.
Book design by Christopher Stengel

ALSO BY DAN POBLOCKI

The Book of Bad Things

The Haunting of Gabriel Ashe

The Nightmarys

The Stone Child

The Mysterious Four #1: Hauntings and Heists

The Mysterious Four #2: Clocks and Robbers

The Mysterious Four #3: Monsters and Mischief

This book is dedicated to Keira Fromm, my earliest ghost-hunting accomplice, and to Caroline McKeown, a fellow enthusiast of abandoned places. Thank you both for your friendship and inspiration.

PROLOGUE

EVERY TOWN HAS ITS SHARE OF SECRETS. And when whispered by children in the dead of night, some secrets become stories. They percolate and brew and change. Sometimes, under special circumstances, the stories become legends, destined to survive even as the children who share them grow up and move on.

In a town called Hedston, a ruined building called Graylock Hall stood in the state forest like an enormous funeral monument. It had once been a notorious psychiatric hospital housing almost one thousand patients. Local kids referred to it as "the asylum in the woods," and most of them knew well enough to stay away. Since its closing, the secrets contained within the hospital's walls had given rise to a frightening legend of madness and murder. If you'd grown up nearby, the subject of that legend — a nurse who had worked the graveyard shift — would have haunted your nightmares from an early age.

It started with a storm.

Late one night while the hospital was still in operation, the building lost electricity in the midst of a summer thunderstorm. During the blackout, one of the patients from the youth ward went missing. The next morning, the staff found the girl's body — drowned, bloated, and blue — facedown in the reeds at the water's edge.

Then, several months later, a second patient drowned — another storm, another power outage. Some of Graylock's staff grew suspicious of the nurse who had been on duty during both accidents, but they said nothing. After a third drowning, the staff wished they hadn't kept their fears secret.

Three children lost. Three bodies discovered at the water's edge — small limbs tangled in lake weed, eyes staring blindly at the pale morning sky.

The people of Hedston refused to believe that the deaths were a coincidence. And so they arrested the nurse who'd worked the graveyard shift, claiming that the madness of the place had infected her — that she had decided death was the only way to end the suffering of the children in her charge. To add to the townspeople's horror, a day after her arrest, the police discovered the nurse's body hanging from a bedsheet that she'd tied to the bars of her cell.

With the nurse's death, the truth of the matter would remain her secret, a secret that became a story, a story that became a legend.

Within a few short years, the hospital was shut down. Graylock Hall was left to rot, but in the town of Hedston, the tale of Nurse Janet lived on.

And they say that, inside the abandoned building, a woman in white still wanders the corridors, her thick-heeled shoes click-clacking against the tile as she follows at an arm's length behind anyone who dares intrude. When she catches you, she sticks you with her needle, then drags you outside to the water's edge, down to the deep tangles of clutching lake weed.

They say she smiles as she holds you under — her face blurred as you stare up through the silvery surface, her teeth glistening white — delighted to continue her murderous quest to end the suffering of the insane. For who but those with their own touch of madness would dare enter the asylum in the woods and pursue its terrible secrets?

Everyone knows you'd have to be crazy to do something like that.

PART ONE

HIDEAWAY

CHAPTER
ONE

Sitting on the porch steps of his aunts' Victorian house, Neil Cady clutched a small satchel in his lap and waited for his new friend, Wesley Baptiste, to arrive. Neil had found the bag at the back of the pantry in his aunts' kitchen and knew it would be perfect for exploring Graylock Hall. Inside, he'd stashed a small flashlight for the shadows, one of his sister's bobby pins for picking locks, a bottle of water, some plastic sandwich bags for collecting evidence, his digital camera, and a notebook and pen.

The night before, Wesley had told him the legend of Nurse Janet. Even after hearing the dire warning to "keep out of Graylock . . . or else!" that concluded the tale, Neil wanted nothing more than to get inside the asylum in the woods to see for himself what the fuss was about.

When it came to ghosts, spirits, and spooky things, Neil considered himself an expert. He and his friends back in New Jersey knew how to create a Ouija board with poster board and a Sharpie marker, how to capture a spirit on film, how to recognize the prickly feeling you get in supposedly haunted places. These all took practice to master, but Neil had some good mentors. His favorite show, *Ghostly Investigators*, was on every Friday night. Neil had not missed an episode since the show had debuted two years ago. The hosts, Alexi and Mark, had three great tips for optimizing data collection during a ghost hunt: Keep your batteries fresh, your mind open, and your underwear clean.

"Waiting for the bus home?"

Neil turned to find his older sister, Bree, standing behind him in the doorway.

"Har-har," said Neil, swiveling away from her. "So funny, you are."

"I don't think it's coming," said Bree, continuing the joke. She stepped out onto the porch, pretending to gaze down the quiet street. A strong breeze shook the leaves in the woods across the road, as if a phantom vehicle were passing by on its way to an unfathomable destination. After a moment, Bree sat down next to him. "Seriously, though, why do you look like you're going somewhere? Aunt Claire and Aunt Anna told us to wait here for them."

"Aunt Claire mentioned that they'd 'be right back.' Neither of them said a thing about waiting for them."

His sister pursed her lips. "They're picking up groceries to cook us dinner tonight. The waiting was *implied*. I don't want to get on their bad side after only two days up here."

"I've got plans," said Neil softly. *The more time I spend around the aunts, the more I think about Mom.* He kept the thought to himself.

"Plans?" Bree squinted at him, as if to scold him. "Oh, well, you've *got plans*. Sor-*ry*."

Frustrated, Neil was about to shout out the truth — *I need to think about something else!* — when she gently touched his arm.

"You're not the only one having a hard time with all of this. Come on." Bree tilted her head at the door behind her. "Let's watch TV."

"I'm not having a hard time with anything," Neil lied. "I just don't feel like moping around when we have a whole new town to explore."

"You're skipping out on the aunts to explore Hedston?" Bree's tone conjured a picture in his mind of the run-down main street he'd first encountered a couple days ago. The polluted river smelled a bit like old coffee; a short, yellow waterfall poured over a concrete divider near the small bridge at the town's edge. Rusted train tracks — the wooden ties of which were well on their way to a state of rot — crossed through what had once been a thriving business district, and grass had grown so high between the disintegrating planks that when the wind rustled the tall stalks, it almost sounded like a whistle. The sidewalks of Hedston were cracked and crumbling.

Step on a crack... It was a wonder that up here everyone's mother didn't have a broken back.

"Aunt Claire's pie shop is the only thing this place has going for it," Bree continued, resigned. "What else do you and Wesley think you're going to find out there?"

"We're not going into town."

Bree flinched. "Then, where are you going?"

Neil hesitated. "The insane asylum. Graylock Hall?"

"It's a psychiatric hospital," Bree said. "I don't think people call them asylums anymore except in horror movies."

"Wesley says it's haunted. We're going looking for ghosts."

"No way."

"What do you mean, 'no way'?" Neil fumed.

"Give me a break, Neil! In what world do you think it's okay for you to break into an abandoned building? Who knows what toxic stuff is floating around? Never mind what might be hiding in there. Or who."

Neil cringed — he should have just lied. *Why does lying always get such a bad rap?* The thought of an empty building in the woods had been his only incentive to get out of bed that morning. Since Wesley had told him about the hospital the night before, he'd been ecstatic to have a *real* reason to be here in Hedston. It was something to do — somewhere to go, to escape the idea of his parents. Back in New Jersey, his mother was lost in a swarm of anxious thought, trouble that had been sparked by his father's departure earlier that year to pursue a long dreamed of acting career in California.

Neil's parents had created their own hideaways, both real and imagined, and now Neil would too. Like parent, like child. He hoped the mystery of Nurse Janet would be his escape from all this. Thank goodness for nonexistent cell service near the mountains, or else Bree might actually have a chance of stopping him. The aunts were virtually unreachable at the grocery store.

Still, they could turn into the driveway at any moment.

"Since you're so worried about me, why don't you come too?" Neil said, forcing himself to smile, shrugging his shoulders, chuckling a bit.

When his sister raised an eyebrow, he realized he'd laid it on way too thick.

"Nice try." Bree grabbed his arm. "Come on. Inside."

Neil began to pull away, when a sputtering noise came up the driveway. Thin rubber tires kicked up gravel. A boy on a bicycle skidded to a stop. Wesley Baptiste.

"Hey, Neil! You ready?"

Someone else turned off the street and rode swiftly up the path. He stopped beside Wesley and lifted off his helmet. Neil realized instantly who the boy was. Wesley had mentioned an older brother but had said nothing about him coming with them. "This is Eric."

Eric was like a stretched-out version of his little brother — his face longer, his jawbone more angular, his shoulders wider. His eyes and skin were slightly darker than his little brother's, but it was obvious that the two boys came from the same parents. Straddling his bike, Eric waved a curt salute.

"His band kicked him out this morning," said Wesley, "so he decided to tag along. He plays guitar."

Eric's smile dropped away, and he threw a death glare at his little brother. "They didn't *kick* me out," he said, almost to himself. "I quit. They're a terrible band."

Bree stood, moving in a single fluid motion, like a dancer lifting delicately off a stage. Neil watched as she smoothed her long brown hair and straightened the hem of her baby blue T-shirt. "I play the viola," she said. As the words escaped her mouth, she blushed. Eric simply stared at her. "So . . . I know how hard it can be to work with other musicians — an orchestra, in my case, which is slightly different. But still . . ." She cleared her throat. "Maybe I should come with you guys too," she said, glancing at Neil. "I mean, it's probably a good idea to have some adults there. For safety's sake." Neil pressed his lips together. He hated when she made him feel like a kid, even though she was a mere four years older than him. "I just need to grab my sneakers. Wait for me?" She dashed back into the house, not listening for an answer, slamming the screen door behind her.

"Who's an adult?" Wesley said to Neil. "I thought you said Bree was only sixteen."

"Give the girl a break," Eric said softly. "She's looking for an adventure. Just like you guys."

Neil raised an eyebrow as Wesley smiled at him.

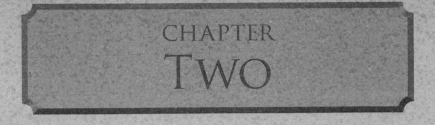

CHAPTER
TWO

THE BAPTISTE BROTHERS LEANED THEIR BIKES against the side of the porch. Since Bree didn't have a bike of her own and was scared to ride on any of their handlebars, they'd all have to walk. Neil was annoyed, but at least Bree had given up her goal of keeping him from going to Graylock.

Taking a right at the end of the driveway, the small group hiked along the side of the road. The summer sunlight filtered between the tree trunks, making stripes of shadow at their feet. Cicada song rose and fell in nearly deafening waves. The beauty of the afternoon clashed with the group's intention — a fact that was not lost on Neil, who grew increasingly excited with every step. He could almost feel the presence of the building in the woods, waiting for him. "How much farther?" he asked.

"There's a turnoff just ahead," said Eric. "I can't believe how close your aunts live to this place."

"I can't believe Neil hadn't heard of Graylock until I told him about it last night," said Wesley.

"Me neither!" said Bree, skipping forward so she could walk beside Eric. "I mean, I've known about it for years." After a moment of uncomfortable silence, she added, "How did you all meet?"

"Well, Wesley's my little brother," said Eric, with a smirk. "We go way back."

Bree blushed. "Yeah, I got that. But where did you find Neil, Wesley?"

"The library, of course," said Wesley.

A couple days before, when Neil and Bree had arrived at their aunts' house, the first thing they all did together was visit the pie shop. After eating an amazingly gooey piece of shoofly pie in the shop's cozy café, Neil thanked Claire and Anna and asked if he could stroll down Tulley Avenue, the main road running through Hedston.

He hadn't been able to get his mother's tearstained face out of his head. *I just need some time alone, honey,* she'd informed him only a week earlier. Her sister, Claire, had offered to take Neil and Bree for the summer. Hedston was several hours north of their home in New Jersey. Neil's uncle, Felix, lived closer, in a studio apartment in Jersey City. But he also worked late in New York City. They would have been alone all day and most evenings, and at night, they'd have had to cramp onto a small fold-out couch.

So instead, Neil had escaped up to the country with his sister, only to find unlimited time to think about all the horrible things his brain insisted he remember. Neil now understood: You cannot escape from yourself. He also understood that his brain wasn't so different from his mother's.

That first day in Hedston, Neil walked up and down Tulley Avenue several times, kicking stones out of his way, plucking leaves off shrubs in front of shabby-looking cottages, humming nonsense songs to himself.

Neil had passed the library twice before he noticed a boy sitting on the top step, staring intensely off into the distance. Neil turned toward where the boy was gazing, but all he could see was a dip in the road that revealed a wooded hillside, the leaves of the far trees blowing in the breeze.

"Do you see him?" the boy asked from the top of the stairs. After a few seconds, Neil realized that the boy was talking to him.

"See who?"

"The Green Man," said the boy, with a smile. He wore a white T-shirt with what looked like a neon-purple Popsicle stain dribbled down the front. His frizzy black hair lay half-curled like a mop on top of his head.

Neil looked back across the street, trying to find someone who might fit the description of "Green Man." But there were only trees, hills, sky, clouds.

"Don't tell me you've never heard of a Green Man," said the boy, waving for Neil to come up the stairs. "You can probably see him better from here." Neil followed, sitting next to the boy on the top step. "Green Men are from Irish folklore. They're a kind of forest spirit."

"Forest spirit?" Neil asked. "Is that like a ghost?"

"Not really," said the boy. "More like . . . an entity."

An entity? Neil found himself amused and disturbed at the same time. The boy sounded a little crazy.

"Want me to teach you to see him?"

"Okay," Neil said, remembering Alexi and Mark, trying to stay open-minded.

"It's mostly a mental thing," said the boy. "First, you've got to relax. Look off at the hillside. Let your vision go fuzzy." Across the small valley was a blur of green. Trees, trees. More trees. "Now," the boy continued, "let the lights and the darks of the leaves leap out."

"Leap out?"

"Just try."

A few seconds later, something strange occurred. Neil didn't know how it happened, but just the act of staring — concentrating — put him in a different kind of place. He could feel the cold stone steps beneath him, the breeze tickling his face, but he felt . . . elsewhere.

"The shadow and light will blur. Look closer. Fall into it. He's right there. In the blur. Look. A face."

The boy was right. Where the shadows retreated into the mass of leaves on the hill, suddenly Neil noticed a pair of eyes blinking, a mouth opening and closing, as if reciting some silent song as the wind blew through the trees.

Neil gasped and then the face was gone. He turned to the boy. "Was that thing real? The Green Man?"

The boy laughed. "*You* saw him, didn't you?" He quieted, and then peered off into the distance again. "You'd be surprised how easily you can find them. Sit and stare at *anything* for awhile . . . it will eventually stare back."

Neil chuckled, pleased to meet someone who might be as weird as himself. He'd definitely seen the face in the trees. If this boy saw it too, then they were in it together. And neither of them were nuts.

The boy smiled to himself, as if the Green Man across the way had suddenly winked at him. "I'm Wesley, by the way."

Neil knew right then that they'd be friends.

By the time Neil had made it back to the pie shop, he found himself looking around at pieces of the town — sidewalk stains, patterns in brickwork, shadows falling across concrete — trying to find hidden life inside all of it. He couldn't help but also think of his parents — how a useful skill such as Wesley's might have given him a clue to the secrets they had kept for so long, secrets to which he still had no satisfying answer.

"Here we are," said Eric, pausing near a gravel road that led into a dense growth of pine. Next to the inconspicuous intersection, hidden by tall weeds and low-hanging branches, a small wooden sign stood atop a thick post: GRAYLOCK HALL — STATE HOSPITAL.

"Notice how it says nothing about crazy people," said Eric, with a smirk. "Totally bland."

"What would you like it to say?" Wesley asked. "'Welcome to the Loony Bin'?"

"Where is it?" Neil asked.

"Way back through the trees," said Eric. "You have to cross a bridge at the end of the long driveway. The main building is on a small island in Graylock Lake. The woods are state property. There's not much else out here." As the group stood at the edge of the path, a gust of wind released needles from high pine boughs swaying over their heads. The needles scattered at their feet. The dark scent of sticky sap hung in the air. "You sure you want to do this?"

"Is it dangerous?" Bree asked.

"Probably," Eric answered with a slight shrug.

Bree sighed and hugged her ribs, as if protecting herself from a chill that didn't exist, but eventually she took the first step onto the gravel road. They all walked in silence for awhile. A couple driveways turned off the thin stretch. Through the dense trees,

Neil could see buildings in the distance. Old houses. He wondered if anyone still lived in them.

"You don't really believe the hospital has ghosts in it," Bree said eventually. "Do you?" She spoke directly to Eric; it was obvious to her how Neil and Wesley felt.

"It's hard not to believe it when so many people claim to have seen her," said Eric.

"Seen *who*?" Bree whispered.

"The nurse."

Neil would have laughed if Wesley hadn't already given him the rundown the day before. Now he listened as Eric recounted it for his sister. Though hearing it for a second time, the story again gave him chills.

"And we're going here . . . *why*?" said Bree, stopping in the middle of the gravel path as Eric finished the tale.

"There's so much to see," said Eric. "After Graylock was closed fifteen years ago, the patients were either moved to other institutions or released. It happened in a hurry. They even left behind charts, specimens . . . medical records!"

Wesley skipped forward. "Tell them about the padded cells with gouge marks in the walls. Or the bloodstains streaking the hallway floors. Or the crayon graffiti drawings that decorate the spiral stairwells."

Neil could tell that Bree was truly frightened — she'd locked her knees and shoved her hands deep into her pockets. If they weren't careful, she might take off in the opposite direction. That would be a disaster — especially if she had the aunts drive out here to pick him up. "He's kidding," said Neil, rolling his eyes.

"Come on," said Eric. He reached out and took her hand. "I might get scared without you." Bree's knees loosened, something sparked in her eyes, and Neil knew they were in the clear. They walked ahead.

Seconds later, Wesley whispered into Neil's ear. "But I *wasn't* kidding."

CHAPTER
THREE

AS THE GROUP APPROACHED THE SMALL BRIDGE, they came to an old metal fence that leaned forward, sagging and rusted. Neil noticed a small space at the bottom. Eric grabbed the chain link and pulled up. The gap opened wider. One by one, Bree, Wesley, and Neil crawled through. Eric followed carefully, pressing himself into the dirty ground so the twists of metal wouldn't scratch.

The path continued across the small concrete bridge, over the algae-coated water where tall reeds wavered, and onto the long, narrow island. Neil marveled at the sight of the hospital grounds. Pine trees lined the road, providing the ever-present shade that Neil somehow had expected to find here. Ahead, visible between the tree trunks, stood a mass of gray stone. A gate. A wall. Neil couldn't tell exactly what he was looking at. Whatever it was, it was covered with a moss so green it appeared poisonous.

"There she is," said Eric. "Graylock Hall."

They walked in silence. The road led to a circular turnaround in front of the building. On the other side of the circle was the hospital's main entrance — a wide stone staircase that rose toward a recessed entry. Within the shadows of the portal, impenetrable black iron doors were chained shut.

The building was not wide, but each of its three stories seemed to rise taller than the last, so that the place loomed as if it were actually leaning toward them, trying to hypnotize them forward.

A small walking path circumnavigated the hospital. Opposite this trail, the land sloped quickly toward the water. It wasn't difficult for Neil to imagine a patient wandering out into the night and tumbling into the lake. Farther from shore, unimpeded by the shade of the pines, lily pads floated in the sunlight. For a patient who couldn't swim, who was confused or frightened in the first place, Neil imagined that it would have been difficult to escape the tangle of plant stalks and weeds out there.

Taking in the vista, Neil was overwhelmed with a sudden sadness. People had died here. And for the people who had lived, life certainly hadn't been easy — neither inside nor outside of these walls. He had come here hoping to escape from his tangled thoughts, but found himself twisted in new ones.

Neil blinked and pulled out the digital camera, fitting its strap snugly around his wrist. He remembered how Alexi and Mark worked. They always managed to keep a critical perspective and maintain an emotional distance. They never jumped to conclusions. Neil took several pictures to make himself feel better. This was his very own ghostly investigation — a wonderful distraction.

"I think there's a window around the side that we can crawl through," said Eric. "That's what my friend Jamie told me this morning anyway. He's been here before, but I couldn't convince him to come again. Go figure."

"Is Jamie in your band?" Bree asked, following Eric to the left of the hospital's main entrance.

"Nah. I'm not really talking to those guys at the moment." The two walked on. Neil and Wesley hung back.

"Are you sure you're ready for this?" Wesley asked. "Some people think Nurse Janet is totally real."

"Yeah, but ghosts can't hurt you," said Neil.

"Where'd you get that idea?"

Neil thought for a few seconds. Had Alexi or Mark ever actually said that? "I'm not sure. Makes sense though. Ghosts don't have bodies. So how would they be able to touch you?" Wesley said nothing. Neil worried Wesley didn't believe him. "The Nurse Janet story is creepy, but I doubt her ghost would really be able to drag anyone down to the lake. Even if she *was* totally psycho."

"There are other ways to hurt people."

"Like how?"

Wesley pointed to his temple, right next to his small brown ear. "What if they can get in here somehow?"

"In your head?" asked Neil. He thought of his mother, of her crying fits, of her silences, her unrecognizing face. He ruminated upon that shadow person he imagined lurking inside himself, and his stomach clenched. Maybe it had been a mistake to come here.

A voice called out from around the stone wall. "Are you guys coming or what?" It was Eric.

"Yes!" Neil answered. Moving forward would keep the memory of his parents in the back of his mind, instead of front and center.

Neil and Wesley found Bree helping Eric into what looked like a tall basement window that met a slight depression in the ground. The glass had been smashed in. The grass at the base of the wall came up to Bree's knees. She held Eric's hands as he lowered himself inside. When Bree realized that the two boys were standing behind her, she blushed, looking like an accomplice to a crime. *And it is a crime*, thought Neil, *isn't it?*

"There's a table down here!" Eric called from the darkness beyond the window. "Looks pretty sturdy." The sound of wooden legs scraping against a gritty floor echoed out of the building. Then Eric's face appeared inside, at the bottom of the frame. "Here." He waved. "You can just climb on in now. The drop isn't far."

Bree breathed deeply, then sat down and scooted herself forward. From inside, Eric reached out and helped her. Wesley followed. Neil glanced around, making sure no one was watching them before he too crouched in the tall grass. He sat on the ledge of the window, and for the first time, he caught a glimpse of the hospital's inside.

Dusty light revealed a wide wooden floor, a tall ceiling. Bolted high on opposite walls . . . were those basketball hoops? Had they found a gymnasium? Weird. And kind of cool.

Neil lowered his bag inside. Below, his sister held it for him. Then he dropped to the table. The safety of the sunlight remained outside. Inside, the world had turned to shadows and dust.

CHAPTER
FOUR

A THICK LAYER OF DIRT CAKED THE FLOOR. Shards of glass glimmered in the dim light at the group's feet. A slimy green stripe of mildew and moss clung to the wall, dripping down from the makeshift entry. A shadowy horizontal line, about five feet high, stretched around the room, reminding Neil of a grimy bathtub ring.

Nature was slowly reclaiming the building. The once-glossy flooring was warped from water damage. Rain had repeatedly flooded the room during years of neglect. Paint peeled from the ceiling, bubbled and hanging in long strips like streamers at a party. Great chunks of plaster had fallen indiscriminately around the room, littering the court with even more debris. *Playing a ball game here today would involve a strange obstacle course*, Neil thought. *What penalties would you acquire for tripping over a raised board?*

Bree tapped Neil's shoulder and held out his bag. She stared at him silently.

"You okay?" he asked her, reaching inside the satchel and removing his camera again. He realized that he actually appreciated that she'd come along . . . even if it *was* simply because Eric — a cute boy! — had shown up.

"Where to?" she asked, glancing around the ruined room.

"Neil wants his evidence," said Wesley. "If Nurse Janet haunts the youth ward, we should try to find her there."

Neil raised his camera and snapped a few shots of the gymnasium. Then he waved for the other three to line up. "Smile!" he said as the flash lit up the room.

They wandered. The labyrinthine hallways were dark, some of them almost pitch-black. Neil's flashlight came in handy as they stumbled through doorways, past overturned gurneys and dust-encrusted wheelchairs, and up a narrow flight of stairs. Spiders and insects scurried away from the sudden glare. Neil kept his body tight, his limbs close to his torso, in case something reached out to grab him.

The group had no idea where they were headed. Neil took comfort in snapping pictures along the way. Alexi and Mark always said: *You never know what the camera might pick up.*

"Where are the padded rooms?" asked Wesley. "And blood. I don't see streaks anywhere."

"Yeah," said Bree. "What about graffiti in the stairwells? I thought this place was going to be much creepier. It just seems dirty." Neil held his tongue. From the way she was scooting ahead to be close to Eric, he knew she was nervous. "And if I wanted to be scared of dirt, I'd just look under Neil's bed back in New Jersey. I swear, he's got some hostile dust bunnies."

Now she'd gone too far. "Such a comedian," said Neil. "Maybe I should tell them what I found under your bed last month."

"Don't you dare!"

"I don't believe every story I hear," said Eric smoothly, keeping his voice low. "About this place especially. Maybe there *are* no padded rooms. No bloody hallway streaks. But we haven't even seen a tenth of what this place has to offer yet."

Neil took a deep breath and let it out slowly.

"Look," said Wesley, pointing at a sign that was posted on a nearby wall.

Activity Rooms	←
Adult Ward	→
Cafeteria	→
Exercise Yard	←
Youth Ward	←

"Sweet," Eric said. "Maybe the cafeteria is serving snacks. I could totally go for some nachos right now."

Bree chuckled.

Wesley grabbed his brother's sleeve and tugged him in the opposite direction. "Come on, Eric. You're gonna drive Neil crazy."

As they all headed toward the youth ward, that word hung in the air, collecting dust.

Crazy.

Neil took the lead, trying to outrun it.

Worn linoleum covered the floors, and cracked white ceramic lined the walls. The hallways in this section of the building were long and straight. The group's footfalls echoed, ringing in their ears, as every step brought them farther away from their entry point and closer toward what they hoped was their goal. They walked without speaking — as if out of respect for the former occupants. Or out of plain old fear. Maybe a little of both.

Neil marked down each turn in his notebook so that they would have a clue about how to get back out.

He understood quite well how clues worked. His mother, Linda, had been fine until January, when his father had announced he was moving out. Marriages ended all the time, Neil understood, but usually there was some big sign that something was wrong — fights mostly, at least according to those of his friends whose parents had split up. But Neil's clues had come during the strange silences at dinners, or nights when he listened to his mom cry herself to sleep.

Neil closed his notebook. Eventually, the group came to a double door. Through panes of glass that were embedded with crisscrossed wire, they saw the doors led to a large, rectangular room. Sunlight spilled in from tall windows along the opposite wall. Eric pulled on the door handle. A sweet, almost nauseating scent escaped. Wesley sneezed.

After they'd all slipped inside, Bree gasped. On the far left side of the room, a table had been set up as if for some sort of party. A festive cloth — faded blue with whitefaced, grinning clowns — covered the table. Someone had arranged paper plates for a large gathering that seemed to have never occurred. A cake, which looked as though it had solidified underneath its faded pink sugar coating, perched in the center on a small silver stand. A large chunk of it was missing. Several conical party hats littered the floor. And a banner had half-fallen from its place on the wall beyond. It read HAPPY BIRTHDAY.

"Weird," Bree whispered, entranced. She bent to pick up one of the hats from the floor but stopped herself, as if she needed to protect the site in the same way an archeologist would.

"Still hungry?" Neil said as Eric stepped forward. "It's not nachos, but petrified cake might be yummy too." Eric ignored him, turning slowly in a circle, taking in the room, mesmerized by what they'd found.

The youth ward.

Toys lay scattered on the floor. The glass eyes of a wooden rocking horse stared out at nothing in particular, waiting blithely for its next rider. An incomplete jigsaw puzzle sat on the floor a few feet from the windows, its image bleached nearly white by the southern sunlight that had moved slowly across the room every day for the past fifteen or so years. To the right of the windows, a shelving unit was packed with a large variety of dolls and stuffed animals, some of which had inexplicably toppled to the ground, lying like corpses at a murder scene. The rest of the creatures seemed to wait, as if their dormant lives could be reactivated by someone picking them up and offering to play.

When Neil raised his camera and flashed another picture, his fellow explorers all exclaimed their version of a yelp. "Sorry," Neil whispered.

"It seems like everyone left in such a hurry," said Bree.

"Maybe once the staff knew they were being forced out," Eric suggested, "they realized that packing up, or even cleaning, would be pointless."

"Still . . . ," said Bree, unable to comprehend what had gone on here during the institution's final days.

Neil understood what she was feeling — it was as though they had stumbled upon a car crash, its victims long gone. This must be what Alexi and Mark experienced in places like this. He lowered his camera and simply observed the stillness, listened to the silence.

Outside, a duck settled noisily upon the lake, quack-quacking, splashing the water's surface with frantic wings.

"What's upstairs, I wonder?" said Wesley. He'd noticed what looked like a large cage in the far corner of the room, next to the party table. Inside white mesh bars, a set of metal steps stretched up into the ceiling.

"Or downstairs," said Neil. Underneath the "up" staircase, blocked by another wire door, more steps disappeared into the floor.

"Look," said Eric, pointing at a sign on the wall.

Dormitory   ↑ Up
Boiler/ Exit   ↓ Down

"That's where they slept," said Wesley.

"Wouldn't hurt to check it out," said Bree. And suddenly, Neil wished she hadn't made that assumption. The darkness — both upstairs and down — seemed to hum at him tunelessly.

"The cage door looks locked," said Eric as Wesley reached out to grab at the grating. But the door squeaked open. Wesley raised an eyebrow, and Eric shrugged.

Neil grappled with his flashlight and flicked it back on. Beyond the lip of the highest stair, another hallway stretched off into inky darkness. "Guess I'm first," he said unsurely as he moved away from the comforting sunshine of the common room.

Once he'd made it to the top, he turned around to make sure his friends had followed. Their wide eyes reflected his own nervousness. The hallway up here unsettled him more than any area they'd already wandered through. Maybe it was that multiple doors stood in opposite walls every few feet, closed and blocking out whatever light they might otherwise have let in. Maybe it was the curve of the hallway at the end of the corridor that appeared to lead off into nothingness. Maybe it was the intimacy of knowing that this was where the patients had slept, lived, dreamed — patients who had not been much older than Neil. He wondered what they had done to end up here. What had been wrong with them?

When his father had left, something shifted inside Linda, as if she'd become possessed by the spirit of someone else. This new mom frightened Neil; he didn't know her at all. She cried. She screamed. She was silent for hours at a time. *New* Mom's emergence made him wonder if he had a shadow person hiding inside him too. He certainly felt like it sometimes — especially when he thought of his parents. What would happen if the shadow decided to come out? Would that mean he was crazy? Would they send him away to a place like Graylock Hall?

When you come back, I'll be better, she'd told Neil finally. *I promise. I've got a lot of work to do.* Neil understood it wasn't the kind of work you got paid for. *You* paid for *it*.

The others stepped forward, crossing Neil and his flashlight. Eric opened the closest door. Sunlight flooded the immediate hallway. He noticed a placard on the wall. This was room number 1. Inside, dust motes swirled above a small twin bed, where a rumpled and stained pillow sat propped against a greenish-brownish wall. The room itself was not much bigger than the bed itself, and the space was otherwise empty.

Were they all the same? Neil wondered. He couldn't imagine spending ten minutes alone in this room, never mind a night, or a week, a month, a year.

More . . .

"Guys," he whispered. "Maybe we shouldn't —"

But the group had separated, opening different doors as they moved down the hallway. Neil gave in and comforted himself by taking pictures as he drifted from room to room. The walls in one had been decorated with posters, mostly of cute baby animals with not-quite-witty slogans printed underneath the images. One poster instructed a kitten who was dangling precariously from a tree branch to HANG IN THERE, BABY.

When Neil peeked his head back outside into the hallway, he realized he was alone.

In the hallway behind him, where he and his friends had opened the doors, light filled the space. But that far bend in the corridor ahead remained as shadowed as before. If everyone had gone on without him, why had none of them opened the doors like they'd done before?

A quiet shuffling sound came from the darkness.

Neil's flashlight provided a tiny bit of comfort as he made his way around the bend. His light revealed another long passage that extended farther than the beam. A door about halfway down the new hall was open; however, no sunlight streamed forth. If the room had a window, something was blocking it. A curtain. A board. He crept closer.

"Hello?" His voice sounded louder than he'd meant it to. No one answered. That shuffling sound continued. Soft soles on a slick floor. Neil paused, his skin prickling. "Hello?" He whispered this time. Again, no answer. He tried to take another step forward, but he found he couldn't move. His muscles felt like Jell-O, his shoes like cement bricks.

Still holding the flashlight in place, he raised his camera to adjust the settings, preparing to snatch a hurried shot in case something unpleasant suddenly appeared before him. Neil forced his feet forward, dragging his sneakers against the tile, the rubber soles squealing their opposition.

He came to the edge of the door frame. The placard on this open door read 13. Lucky number 13. Leaning forward with the flashlight, Neil peered around the corner.

A white figure stood in the center of the small bedroom. She seemed to be staring at the shuttered window. Her long brown hair hung almost halfway down her back. She clenched her fists at her sides. But she did not turn, not even when Neil let out a small groan.

He'd found Nurse Janet.

CHAPTER
FIVE

THE FIGURE SWAYED SLIGHTLY, and Neil immediately realized his mistake. She was not dressed in white, but the bright flashlight had made it seem so.

Bree was wearing the same blue T-Shirt and shorts as when they'd left the aunts' house. That was how he recognized her.

Still, something was strange here. Hadn't she heard him calling? "Bree . . . ," Neil said quietly, calmly. She made no sign that she'd heard him. "Bree," he said, louder this time. Again, nothing. This was weird. Too much like his mom. Neil had worried about his own shadow person; should he have been worrying about Bree too?

Neil stepped through the doorway. Even though the room was about the same size as the other ones, this one felt smaller. Claustrophobic. As if the walls were moving in on him.

He touched Bree's shoulder. But she did not turn.

Instead, she simply said, "There's something about this room. . . ." Her voice sounded foggy, as if she'd just woken from a deep sleep.

"Let's go." Neil's flashlight flickered. A flash of panic crackled his skin. Shadows leapt out from the walls momentarily before retreating swiftly back into place. Bree finally turned to look at him, but her eyes were blank, as if she were peering through him. Several seconds passed before she blinked and appeared to recognize him. "Come on," Neil tried again. "We've got to find Wesley and Eric."

"Who?"

Neil clutched the flashlight even harder and noticed his hand shaking. He answered slowly, carefully. "We came here with my friend Wesley Baptiste and his brother, Eric. Remember?" Under different circumstances she'd have poked his chest, thinking he was teasing, but now she merely nodded, thankful for the reminder. Neil reached out to take her hand, but she stepped backward toward the blackened window.

"This room . . . ," she said, glancing over her shoulder.

"What about it?" Neil said, frustrated, as he moved toward the doorway. At that moment, he only wanted to get back down to the common room.

"Shh." Bree cocked her head, listening to what sounded like silence. "Do you hear that?"

A chill wrapped Neil's body, head to toe. "Hear what?"

"Whispering."

The flashlight winked out. Darkness came like eyes shut tight. Neil and Bree collided with each other before bouncing away. They both screamed, then froze, paralyzed by fear and a dizzying sense of disorientation.

"We're fine," Neil said a second later. "The battery died." He flicked the flashlight switch on and off, trying without success to milk the last of the juice from it. They were blind. After shoving the device into his bag, he managed to find Bree's hand in the darkness. "Come on —"

WHAM.

The room shook. Neil felt himself fall backward, tripping and landing on a damp mattress. Bree's voice lifted dramatically, "What was *that*?"

"I don't know," he said, standing. "Let's go." He dashed toward the doorway, only to meet a blossom of pain — his forehead and his nose felt as if they'd exploded. He groaned. Something wet dripped over his lip. He stuck out his tongue and tasted blood.

"The door must have slammed shut," said Bree, a disembodied voice beside him. Back to normal. "Are you okay? That sounded bad."

He wiped at his face, the warm liquid coating the back of his hand. "I'm bleeding."

"Your nose?"

"Yeah."

"Pinch it. Up near the bridge." Bree touched his shoulder. Neil heard her fidgeting with the doorknob. "This thing is stuck." Neil's entire face throbbed, but this news made the rest of his body feel numb. "Can you help?" Bree asked.

Ignoring the pain, Neil reached out blindly. He grabbed the knob, but it wouldn't turn. Even when he threw his weight backward, the door refused to give. "Are we trapped in here?"

"Wesley!" Bree cried. "Eric? We know you're out there!" She listened to the silence for several seconds. "This is *not* funny! Let us out!" She pounded on the metal door. It reminded him of thunder. They could use some lightning.

The camera! It had a flash. Maybe there was a latch on the door that they'd missed.

He grabbed at the camera, which still hung from his wrist, but lost precious seconds as it slid from his grip, his fingers trembling and slick with his own blood. Finally, he clutched the camera's metal casing and held the device out before him. "Stand back," he said. He pressed the shutter button, and cold light burst inside the small room. When the afterimage of the flash died down, the room seemed darker still. Even if he had seen the details of the door-knob, he wouldn't have been able to figure it out now. "Useless," he whispered.

"Not useless," said Bree. "Turn on the view screen. It's got to give off a bit of light."

Licking his lip, tasting the coppery liquid there, Neil blindly pressed a couple buttons. The screen on the back of the camera glowed blue. He held it up to the doorknob. It appeared plain, round, silver. If there was a lock at all, it was on the outside. "What the heck! How are we supposed to —"

Someone shushed him.

But it wasn't Bree.

Wide-eyed, he and his sister stared at each other, their faces lit by the camera from below. Slowly, they turned. At the other side of the room, near the window, a dark shape stood completely still. It looked like one of their own shadows. Neil knew this was impossible. The camera's light was *between* them and the shape. Their shadows should have been cast on the door behind them. Shaking, unable to speak, Neil held up the camera, trying to see who was there.

The figure shifted forward. In the dim light, Neil made out some faint details. Long dark hair. Clothed in a light dress, pos-sibly a uniform.

Neil tried to scream, but he couldn't. He couldn't move. Couldn't breathe. Couldn't blink. Even his bloody nose felt as if it had stopped flowing.

Then, just like the flashlight, the camera died.

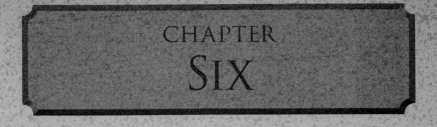

CHAPTER
SIX

Something shoved Neil and Bree forward. The floor tilted. The darkness spiraled. They were falling. Spinning.

But no . . .

The door had merely opened with a swift jolt, knocking into them, sending them off balance. Neil took a step and caught himself.

"What are you guys doing in here?" Wesley's voice came from the hallway. A sliver of dim light broke the curtain of shadow.

Without thinking, Neil yanked the door the rest of the way open. He grabbed his sister's arm and together they leapt out of the room. "Run!" he called to Wesley, who stood momentarily stunned behind them before springing forward. The trio sprinted toward the bend in the corridor, where daylight greeted them like a parent waiting with open arms. They raced toward the stairs. Neil did not look back.

Memories of the Nurse Janet story flickered through his head, like old film from a loud projector, and all he could think of now was her strong hand reaching for his collar. At any moment, he would be caught, choked. As his lower body continued to race forward, his feet would flip upward. He'd fall flat on his back, looking at the ceiling as her pale face came closer and closer, glaring down at him as she —

"Watch out!" Bree grabbed Neil's arm just as he was about to topple headfirst off the top stair. He swung out and clasped the railing, pinning himself against the wall.

Rattled as he was, Neil managed to peer back into the darkness at the corridor's bend. His heart galloped; his lungs burned. His eyes scanned the distance for any movement, anything at all. But nothing was there . . . nothing he could see anyway. "Can we not stop here, please?" he said.

"Are you okay?" said Wesley, following Neil and Bree briskly down the stairs. "You're bleeding, Neil."

"I ran into the door back in that room."

"I heard you guys shouting. Did you see something?"

At the bottom of the stairs, Neil finally found his breath. The sunlight had sunk to a position where it hit the lake and reflected golden light all around the common room.

"I don't know what we saw," Bree said. "Where's your brother?"

"I'm here." Eric came through a doorway on the other side of the cake table. He was holding what looked like a brown file folder. "I found an office. You would not *believe* the things they left behind in this place." When he saw the state of the trio, his eyes grew wide. "What happened?"

"Don't ask," said Neil. "We're leaving."

"Really?" said Eric. "But it looks like things are starting to get good."

"You've been down here for a while?" Bree asked with a scowl.

Eric nodded slowly, wearing an almost obnoxious expression that said, *What's your problem?*

"Someone is upstairs," said Bree, "in one of the bedrooms. She tried to lock me and Neil inside."

"Nurse Janet," said Wesley unsurely.

"No way," said Eric, starting past them toward the staircase. Wesley grabbed his arm. Eric flung him away. "I wanna check it out for myself." He paused, and then added, "I can't wait to tell the band about this."

"They kicked you out!" Wesley shouted.

"You don't know what you're talking about." Eric yanked the mesh door open and climbed the steps two at a time. He disappeared into the opening at the ceiling.

Bree shook her head. "Forget him. I'm not spending another minute in this place."

Wesley blinked. "We can't leave him up there."

"Why not?" said Bree. "He's happy to leave us down here." Her cheeks flushed red. Neil could see that all the charm she'd collected from Eric earlier had evaporated. No one messed with Bree, Neil knew. Eric would learn. "You can stay, Wesley, but I'm taking Neil with me."

Neil sighed. "But —"

Wesley held up his hand. "You're right." Listening to the silence from upstairs, he added, "He can be a real jerk sometimes." He called out, "Meet us outside, Eric!"

They didn't receive an answer.

The three headed back through the door of the youth ward into the long hallway, running in the direction of the crumbling gymnasium — at least, that's where they thought they were headed. Even though Neil had marked every turn they'd made, after what had happened in room 13, his sense of direction was now screwed up — not good, since they were heading into some very dark places without a working flashlight.

"Which way?" asked Bree at an intersection of two hallways that looked exactly like the last one they'd come to.

"Maybe there's a sign like before," said Wesley, peeking around a corner.

"But don't we have to go down some stairs eventually?" Neil asked. In fact, through an open doorway up ahead, there was a stairwell. The group crept forward. The passage led down into complete darkness. "Is this the one we came up?"

"I think so," said Wesley.

"There's got to be another way out," said Bree. "One that doesn't involve us wandering around a pitch-black maze. What if we just keep going straight ahead on this floor instead?"

"We could try that," said Wesley. "I mean, it's not like we're trapped in here or anything."

"You're right," Neil answered quickly. The memory of the blindness he'd experienced upstairs swept through him. He knew he'd have nightmares tonight. Best to remain logical, levelheaded. Like Alexi and Mark. He stepped back from the stairwell and nodded down the corridor. "Let's try this way. At the very least, if we come to a window, we can climb out. It shouldn't be too far of a drop."

"I remember the second story being pretty high up," said Bree. "And after everything else, I really don't feel like breaking my ankle today."

Neil shrugged. Glancing back down the stairwell, he said, "Well, there's our other option." The darkness seemed to swell near the bottom steps like black floodwater rising steadily.

"You're right," said Bree. "There's no way —"

"Shh," said Wesley. "Listen."

Then Neil heard it too. From back toward the youth ward, sharp footsteps echoed toward them. *Clip-clip-clip-clip-clip.*

"Eric?" Wesley whispered.

"Eric's wearing sneakers," said Bree. "Isn't he?"

"It's gotta be somebody else," said Neil. The legend said Nurse Janet's heavy heels could be heard throughout Graylock Hall. And judging from the sound, she was getting closer.

CHAPTER
SEVEN

THEY RAN, TRIPPING, COLLIDING WITH ONE ANOTHER. The hallway expanded, seemed to grow. They didn't know where they were headed, but they didn't care, as long as it was away from the sound of the approaching footsteps. Their own footfalls now bounced off the walls. The squeaking of their rubber soles on the cracked linoleum sounded like an old-fashioned drag race, cars skidding on a wet track. For a moment, Neil imagined that was exactly what they were doing — racing. And if they lost . . .

Ghosts can't hurt you, he thought. But Neil's bruised nose continued to throb. His lips still tasted of blood. What if Wesley hadn't been here to open that door? Would Neil and Bree have spent the night here in Graylock Hall? How long would it have taken for someone to come looking for them and how much longer to find them in that obscure upstairs hallway?

Neil sprinted, pumping his arms faster, determined to reach the door that was just ahead, to slam it shut and barricade it from whatever was chasing them.

Bree and Wesley kept up. They all careened through the doorway and found themselves in what at first appeared to be a dead end. Another large room; high-beamed ceilings; an expansive, scratched-up wooden floor. A wide, stone mantel was set deep into the far wall. A fireplace blackened with soot opened like a howl beneath it. This room had once been used for entertaining — rotting leather couches and wide circular tables were pushed against the wall in front of a wall of built-in bookcases. An enormous Persian rug had been rolled up and shoved underneath the row of windows that looked out over the lake.

A loud ruckus erupted from a far corner of the room. Turning, the trio watched in horror as a massive black entity expanded, pulsating and shivery, all the way up to the ceiling.

Wesley screamed.

Moments later, he covered his mouth, attempting to contain his nervous laughter. It was only birds. Several large crows circled overhead, cawing, taunting them, before settling back down near the fireplace mantel.

A strong breeze came in through the cracked windows, where the birds had found entry. Below the windows, beside the carpet, the floor looked as though it was sagging.

Judging by the view of the pines outside, Neil imagined that the gymnasium might be directly below them now. He wiped the remaining blood from his face and stepped farther into the room to get a better look. If they'd entered the hospital just outside, they could easily find their way back to the small bridge and the chain-link fence. They'd only have to wait for Eric to —

Neil swayed forward as the floor dipped. He shouted. The wood gave way and sharp splinters gouged his shin. Panic. Pain. Bree and Wesley rushed forward, but he called out, "Stay back!" They obeyed. He breathed through the stabbing sensations that ran up and down his leg. "The entire floor could give out."

"Then, *you* get away from there too!" Bree cried.

The floor began to creak. Neil imagined a wide wooden mouth opening up and swallowing him. It would be a long drop to the gymnasium floor below.

Neil carefully sat and pulled his leg from the sharp edges of the small hole. As soon as he'd gotten himself out, he plucked several long splinters from the raw wound. He tried to brush away some of the dust and dirt from his skin, but already the pain had begun to magnify. His skin had split deeply in several places. It was tender. Starting to swell and bead with blood. He felt hands on his shoulders. Looking up, he saw Bree. She slowly pulled him away from the weak patch of flooring.

"Are you okay?"

"I don't know." The room was spinning. Neil wanted to puke. But he also felt like laughing. Strange. He knew that nothing about this was funny. They'd made a huge mistake coming here. And the question now was: How would they get out?

The birds on the mantel mocked them. *CAW. CAW. CAW. CAW.*

"Oh, shut up," said Wesley, throwing the birds a nasty look. "Can you walk, Neil?"

Neil struggled but managed to stand up. He groaned as the pain seemed to burst his leg into tiny pieces. "I don't know," he said, gasping. "I hope so." Bree stood on one side of him and Wesley on the other. He put his arms around their shoulders. Together, they managed to move toward the possibility of safety near the bookcases.

"What now?" said Bree. "We're going to have to go back to that staircase down the hallway, aren't we?"

"What if Nurse Janet is out there waiting for us?" Wesley asked.

Footsteps echoed near the wall directly behind them. When they turned, one of the tall shelves seemed to shake back and forth. The three were all too surprised to move, to speak. The shelves crept forward, hinged on one side. It was a hidden door. A stone passage appeared. Inside, darkness wheezed at them.

But no . . . it was not a wheezing sound. Something walked. Shoes against stone. Coming toward them.

CHAPTER
EIGHT

A HUMAN SHAPE MATERIALIZED. When it stumbled into the dimming light of the ballroom, it let out a choking sound, as if it hadn't taken a breath in years. Seconds later, when their eyes adjusted and their brains caught up to their imaginations, Bree, Wesley, and Neil realized that this was no mysterious figure.

This was Wesley's brother.

"Eric?" said Wesley. "What are you doing in there?"

Eric glanced up at the group. Taking in the scene of minor carnage — the blood now dripping down Neil's leg, the hole in the middle of the floor, the crows tapping curious claws on the mantelpiece, and the looks of horror on the trio's faces — Eric shook his head in astonishment. "Sheesh. I keep missing all the good stuff," he said.

Bree scoffed. "*Good* stuff? Where have you been?"

He told them. Upstairs, he'd gone farther down the dark hallway, past room 13, twisting and turning through several wings of the hospital, as if in a daze, until he realized he was entirely lost. He'd ended up in an administrative office and stumbled across a dark crack in one of the stone walls. Upon examination, he discovered what appeared to be a clandestine and very dusty stairwell spiraling downward like a castle turret. At a certain point during his descent, he'd heard what sounded like familiar voices. He pushed his weight against a wooden panel and found his brother and his new friends staring at him.

"We need to go," said Bree, barely able to look at him. "Now. Neil is seriously hurt."

"Not seriously —" Neil started, but when she threw him a sharp look, he shut his mouth.

"I think this is the best way out," said Eric, pointing back toward the passage. "It might get us down to the ground level at least."

"Might?" said Bree.

"The gym is right below us, right, Neil?" said Wesley. "We can crawl out the window where we came in."

Once outside, Neil realized that he'd been holding his breath since reaching the gymnasium floor.

As they'd climbed, one by one, through the broken window, he almost expected a booming voice to call out, echoing through the cavernous room, telling them to stop, that they were not allowed to leave. They would turn to find men directly behind them, wearing white coats and Halloween masks with wide plastic grins, carrying straight jackets and leather ankle restraints to bind them and drag them all screaming back up to room 13, where they would finally meet Nurse Janet face-to-face.

But that did not happen.

Of course.

The sun had fallen behind the horizon of trees across the small body of water. It was getting late. The aunts were most certainly waiting for them, worrying. They made their way back toward the small bridge. When Neil had to kneel down and crawl under the gap in the fence, he cried out. The gashes on his legs seemed to open up and wail at him. Wesley pushed him forward, and Bree helped him stand up again. "You need a doctor," said Bree, shaking her head.

"I'm fine," Neil insisted.

Wesley shook his head. "You look like the last survivor in one of those bloody slasher movies. For real."

They ventured back toward the main road. They were all covered in dirt and grime, their hair sweat-slicked to their scalps. The shoulder seam in Bree's formerly cute blue T-shirt had separated, revealing a small scrape. *How did this happen?* Neil wondered.

Neil understood the stories now — why visitors to the hospital in the woods only came out here *once* before deciding that it had been one trip too many. But was this a story he should tell to his friends during lunch at school? They'd think he was crazy. And if they ever found out the truth about his mother's problems, his classmates would surely start telling stories about him too.

Someone stepped out of the woods in front of them, blocking their path to the main road. A tall man. His big head was shaved bald. A long gray beard grew from sunken cheeks. He looked older than the aunts by many years, yet his shoulders were broad, his arms muscular. He wore a black-and-red plaid shirt and dirt-dusted dark jeans.

The group paused. Neil was too exhausted to even react.

The man crossed his arms, his brow crinkled. He looked as if he knew exactly where they had been and what they'd been up to.

But before he could scold them, he seemed to digest their appearance, taking special notice of Neil's bloody leg. He sighed, as if he'd seen this kind of thing before. "Graylock," said the man, his voice low and rough. This wasn't a question and thus gave the group no option to deny the accusation. He shook his head. "When are you all going to learn? It's a dangerous place. Was before they closed it . . . Still is." He nodded at the woods behind him. "I've lived back there for years, and I've seen enough of this nonsense for a lifetime. Always blood. Always. Come on. I'll drive you kids home." He nodded at Neil. "At the rate you're walking, you won't make it before midnight." He turned around and headed toward the building in the distance, the roof of his house barely visible through the thick foliage.

None of them moved or said a word. But Neil knew what they were thinking: Never accept a ride from strangers, a rule that had been drilled into them from infancy.

The man turned back and glared at them. "What's the holdup?"

"We don't know you," said Eric. "Sorry."

"Well, I know you," said the man. "You're the Baptiste boys. I used to work with your father at the mill." He glanced at Bree and Neil. "You must be Anna and Claire's niece and nephew. They told me you were coming up from New Jersey. I'm Andy. I stop at the pie shop every morning for coffee." The group stared at him in shock. "Don't believe me? I can call them right now and tell them what you were all up to out here."

"No!" said Bree. "No, thank you. Please. We don't want to worry them."

"Probably too late for that," said Andy. "How long have you all been playing around out here?" Neil wanted to tell him that they hadn't been playing around at all, that "playing around" was the opposite of what they'd been doing, but neither he nor any of the others said a word. Andy smiled softly, letting them know he was merely poking fun. "Come on. My truck is right up here."

CHAPTER
NINE

CLIMBING INTO THE FRONT SEAT OF ANDY'S PICKUP, Neil cried out in pain. It felt as if someone had replaced his shinbone with a hot iron spike. Sitting behind the wheel, Andy glanced over at Neil's injury. "Maybe I should take you to see Dr. Simon down on Yarrow Street. Your aunts would probably want to do the same thing anyway." Bree, Wesley, and Eric had climbed into the truck bed and could not hear this exchange. Neil didn't know what to say. As much as his leg hurt, he was kind of happy that it was a distraction from the nightmare they'd encountered that afternoon. "I'll drive you by Anna and Claire's," said Andy. "If they're home, they'll take care of it. If not, we're all going to the doctor." Looking down at Neil's leg, he sucked his teeth, wincing dramatically. "Graylock sure can bite."

At the aunts' house, the driveway was empty save for the Baptiste brothers' bikes, which were still propped against the front porch. Andy slowed but didn't stop, zipping toward the center of Hedston, and Neil cringed. Where could the aunts be? Shouldn't they have been home from the grocery store by now? He supposed he deserved to feel terrible. He had done the same thing to them after all — left the house for the asylum in the woods with absolutely no hesitation, no mention of where he was going.

Hadn't Aunt Anna been watching him cautiously since he'd arrived, as if she had something to worry about? If he wasn't more careful, she might talk Aunt Claire into sending him to stay with his uncle in Jersey City, or worse, back home to his mother. He could forget about escaping from thoughts of his parents then.

Five minutes later, after Andy parked in front of a regal-looking white house, Bree hopped over the edge of the truck bed and opened Neil's door for him. "Where are we?" she whispered.

Neil pointed over her shoulder. A small black sign was posted on a slightly tilted pole in the center of the white house's large lawn. It read DR. JULIUS SIMON — FAMILY MEDICINE.

Leading the group up the stone path to the front door, Andy said, "Dr. Simon is an old friend. It's late, but I'm sure he'll see you." Andy tried the knob, but it was locked. He rang the doorbell. A few seconds later, an annoyed-looking elderly woman answered. She wore a floor-length white cotton nightgown — *Strange*, thought Neil, since it was still daylight. When she noticed that Andy was the caller, her scowl softened. "Hi, Maude," he said. "We've got a bit of an emergency here." He turned around and indicated the motley tribe standing behind him. Neil couldn't help but blush. "Can we pull Julius away from *Wheel of Fortune* for a few minutes?"

Maude smiled reluctantly. "He won't be happy. But if it's an *emergency* . . ." Andy pointed at Neil's leg. "My goodness," she said. "That looks bad." Wide-eyed, she stepped aside and held out her hand, indicating that they were free to enter.

She led them down a long hall — the walls of which were covered with dark-blue floral wallpaper — to a small sitting room crammed with a variety of cushy antique chairs. Most of the upholstery was stained or ripped or simply worn-out. Even so, Neil took comfort in getting off his feet as soon as he could. The others sat down too.

"Be right back," Andy said, and followed Maude through another door, leaving them alone in the waiting room.

"I want to call the aunts," said Bree glancing around, looking for a phone.

"They weren't home when we passed by," Neil said. "Maybe they're out looking for us."

"We're so dead," said Bree, plopping down in the chair next to Neil.

"Yeah," said Wesley. "Our mom and dad aren't going to be too happy with us, either."

Eric leaned forward on the couch where he sat with his brother. From the back of his pants, he pulled the file folder he'd taken from the office in the youth ward.

"You *stole* that?" said Bree.

"So?" said Eric. "Nobody else seemed to want it."

Bree sighed. The elation she may have felt at having met him seemed to have finally leaked entirely out of her.

"What's in it?" Wesley asked, peeking over his brother's shoulder.

"Not sure," said Eric. "Doctor's notes. Medical history. Stuff like that." He flipped the folder over and showed them the name that had been typed on the tab: Caroline Crowne. "She was sixteen. The doctor wrote down that she was suffering from 'hysteria.' Whatever that means."

"It means they thought she was too emotional," said Bree. "Lots of women in the eighteen hundreds used to be locked up for simply speaking their minds."

"Yeah," Eric said, "but this girl wasn't locked up in the eighteen hundreds. She seemed to really need help." He opened the

folder and shuffled through several pages. "She'd attempted suicide several times. She was in Graylock for her own protection . . .
at least that's what it says here."

"I can't imagine that being stuck *there* would make anyone feel
less depressed," said Neil.

"Not all mental hospitals are like Graylock," said Bree. "The
one Mom's at is really —"

"Bree!" Neil shouted.

His sister covered her mouth and closed her eyes, as if she
couldn't stand to be in the same room with the words she'd just
spoken.

"Your mom's in a mental hospital?" Eric asked, closing the
folder and placing it on the coffee table.

Neil glared at Bree, who refused to open her eyes. "It's not a
mental hospital," he said. "She goes to a clinic in New Jersey.
Outpatient. Which means she doesn't have to spend the night
there or anything. She's just been . . . upset since our dad moved to
California." He sighed. "It's why we're up here in Hedston. Our
aunts invited us to stay until she's feeling better." He didn't bother
meeting their eyes.

"She'll be fine soon," Bree said. "Everything is going to be
okay."

"I'm sure it will be," said Eric quietly.

A door across the room swung open and hit the wall. A short,
thin man dressed in a white coat breezed into the space. "All righty,
then," he said. "Where's my patient?"

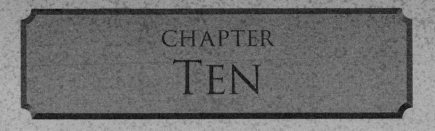

CHAPTER
TEN

IN THE SMALL WHITE ROOM, Neil sat atop crisp paper on the exam table. "So, Andy tells me he found you kids playing in the state woods?" said Dr. Simon.

"He said that?"

The doctor nodded. "What he didn't tell me was how you did this to yourself."

Neil felt his face burn. "I fell." Not a lie. But not exactly the truth.

"I see." The doctor sat on a small stool with wheels. He scooted forward and examined the scrapes on Neil's shin. Then he stood and checked out Neil's nose. The doctor reached for a tissue and handed it over. Neil wiped at his nostrils. Caked blood came away, flecked on the paper. The doctor held a small light up to Neil's eyes. "Well . . . the good news is that none of this looks too serious. We'll clean you up. Bandage your leg."

"What's the bad news?"

Dr. Simon smiled. "Andy said he's heading out to locate Anna and Claire. Knowing how protective those two are, I can assure you that the rest of your night will not be as fun as this."

Neil's lungs tightened. "Really? Are they that strict?"

The doctor smiled and opened a nearby cabinet, fetching a small bottle of iodine. "This may sting a little."

When he'd finished with Neil, Dr. Simon led the way back to

the waiting room, where he rejoined Bree, Wesley, and Eric. "So, I suppose you'll just stay here until your aunts show up."

"Can I use your phone?" Wesley asked the doctor. "My parents are probably wondering where we are." Dr. Simon pointed at another door opposite the one he'd come through.

Bree asked Neil, "Everything okay?"

Dr. Simon nodded his head. "He's fine. Just make sure he changes the bandage tomorrow. Keep it clean. Soap. Water. And a little hydrogen peroxide won't hurt." Then the doctor glanced at the brown file folder on the coffee table. He flinched.

Eric noticed Dr. Simon's reaction and immediately grabbed for the folder. But it was too late. The doctor had seen it. He looked at each of them. Something in his eyes made Neil nervous.

"Where did you get that?" said Dr. Simon, sounding as though he already knew the answer.

"It's not yours," said Eric, "if that's what you were wondering."

"Eric!" Bree whispered, shocked at his rudeness.

"That's *not* what I was wondering actually." Dr. Simon held out his hand. Eric pressed his lips together, and then he handed the folder to the doctor. Dr. Simon tucked his new prize underneath his arm. He stiffened, suddenly businesslike. "You may wait for Anna and Claire here. But I would suggest that there are places in this town where your presence is *not* welcome . . ." He glanced down at Neil's bandages. ". . . as the evidence of your adventure today should remind you."

"You're not going to tell our aunts, are you?" Neil asked.

Dr. Simon smiled — a surprisingly sad expression — and answered, "I hope I won't have to."

CHAPTER
ELEVEN

THEY TOOK ANDY UP ON HIS OFFER TO DRIVE THEM HOME.

Later, after the Baptiste brothers left, Neil sat with Bree at the kitchen table, dutifully chopping broccoli florets. "I'm not going to lie," said Claire, standing at the sink, rinsing a colander filled with stringy pasta. "You had us worried sick." Neil still felt extremely guilty — he hadn't even *tried* to take their feelings into account when he'd set off for Graylock. "Next time you want to go for a walk, just leave us a note. We don't want you to think we're holding you captive here. But, well, Anna does suffer from a heart murmur. You can't cause her any trouble."

Anna stood near the stove, and she leaned far out of her way to bump Claire with her hip. "Leave me and my heart out of this," she said. Her voice sounded jovial, but Neil could read skepticism in her brow. She definitely hadn't bought Andy's story that they'd been surveying the trails behind their house and Neil had tripped on a log.

"We're sorry," said Bree, who sat across the table from Neil, peeling carrots. "I don't know what we were thinking." She tossed him a blameful look.

"The woods are intriguing," said Claire matter-of-factly, "if not a little dangerous. I don't blame you for wanting to explore. We go for long walks sometimes too."

"True," said Anna. "But Claire and I manage to stick to the paths. You guys already know how easy it is to get hurt. It's even easier to get lost." She glanced over her shoulder, throwing Neil and Bree a look that said she knew exactly what they'd been up to. "Just a warning."

After dinner, at Neil's request, the four sat down to watch *Ghostly Investigators*. The aunts had never seen the show before. Tonight's episode was about an abandoned amusement park on the coast of Rhode Island. During the show, Neil described the crew who was involved, how the investigators worked, the tools they used. EMF detectors read fluctuations in electromagnetism — its flashing lights indicated a field change and the possibility of a spirit. Digital recorders captured voices that could not be heard by human ears. Heat-sensitive cameras traced hot and cold spots, another hint that spectral visitors were nearby. The aunts listened skeptically, but seemed to enjoy the episode. At the end, Alexi and Mark remarked that they'd gathered enough evidence to conclude that the park was indeed a haunted place.

"Even after all that," said Anna, "I still can't quite believe. Ghosts? I'm a doubter at heart."

"That's just because you've never seen one," said Claire.

"Have you?" Neil asked Claire. His injured leg was propped up on the couch, at his aunt's insistence.

Claire bunched up her face and shrugged. "I've seen *things*. Nothing I can be sure of. But that's how it works, doesn't it? You get a fleeting glimpse of whatever it is you can't explain."

"Yes," Anna added, "but the difference between us is that if I catch a glimpse of something odd, I find a reason for it. You tend to harp on it until you've convinced yourself: boogeyman." She chuckled, then sighed. "Claire and your mother both put more faith in their imaginations than I do."

At the mention of his mother, Neil flinched. Like parent, like child.

"But what exactly have you seen, Aunt Claire?" Bree asked.

Claire sat silently, looking like she was unsure whether or not to tell the story. Anna crossed her arms and cleared her throat. Claire ignored her and leaned forward. "Have you heard the legend of Graylock? It's the hospital that used to be back in the woods here."

"Yeah," said Neil hesitantly. He avoided Bree's glare. "We've heard stories."

"On our walks in the woods," Claire went on, "I sometimes get the feeling I'm being watched."

"See?" said Anna, throwing up her hands. "Would you call that ghostly?"

"That's not *all*," said Claire. She turned to Anna, her face growing stern. "I never told you this, but once, a couple years ago, when we were near that lake, I swear I saw someone standing at the water's edge. Among the reeds. Just standing there. Looking at us."

"What did the person look like?" asked Neil, trying to contain the sick giddiness that was gathering in his chest.

"She was tall. Long brown hair, I think. Dressed in white."

"*Nurse Janet,*" Neil whispered to himself.

"Who?" Anna asked.

"Uh," he answered, his cheeks turning pink. "I was just think-ing out loud."

Anna squinted at him, looking as if she never wanted him to say that name again. But the expression only lasted for a couple of seconds before softening, "Your leg all right?" she asked. "How about some more pillows?"

When the aunts said good night, Neil brought his borrowed satchel upstairs to his room. He tossed it at a chair beside the bed where it landed with a thunk. The dead flashlight and camera were still inside, along with the other items he'd packed that afternoon. He lay down, his leg stinging, his nose puffy.

Someone knocked at his door. A moment later, Bree peered in at him.

"What's up?" said Neil, even though he knew that the answer was "Plenty."

"Just checking on you."

"I'm fine."

Bree nodded slowly and entered anyway. She sat on the edge of his bed, glancing at his leg, looking as if she needed to tell him something but couldn't speak. Finally, she managed, "I was really scared today, Neil."

He'd felt the same way, but refused to admit it.

"And I'm not just talking about you getting hurt either," she continued. "There was something inside that place . . . something I can't explain."

Neil felt his stomach clench. And though he didn't want to bring it up, there was one question he had to ask. "Why did you go into room 13?" he whispered. He remembered his sister's blank expression when she'd turned to face him.

Bree stared at the ceiling. "That's the thing . . . I don't know. I walked down that hallway, into the dark. I noticed the door was open a crack. I felt like I had to go inside — like it had been my destination all along. And as soon as I did, I felt strange. Like something was trying to talk to me. Something without a mouth . . . without a voice. I felt like I couldn't leave until I heard what it had to say. Then you showed up. And everything went . . . weird."

Neil shivered. "That's totally not what I thought you were going to say. You've always been more like Anna. You don't believe in this stuff."

Bree shrugged. "But you felt it too. Didn't you?"

"I don't know what I felt," said Neil. "It was so strange. We both got confused." Then, as an afterthought, he added, "And you're sure *you* didn't shut the door on us?"

"I think I'd remember doing that."

Neil wasn't satisfied, but he kept his mouth shut. Could it *really* have been a ghost? And if not . . . was the alternative even scarier?

Bree looked at the satchel on the chair beside the bed. "Maybe we can track down some new batteries for the camera tomorrow. Those pictures might show us something we can't remember . . . or didn't see."

"Oh my gosh," Neil said, sitting up on his bed.

Bree stepped away, as if he might explode. "What's wrong?"

"The flashlight. The camera. When we were in room 13, the batteries died almost instantaneously."

"And?"

"According to Alexi and Mark, that's a sign that something is trying to manifest."

"Manifest?"

"Appear. Make itself known. A spirit doesn't have its own energy, so it needs to take energy from other places in order to do stuff."

"Stuff like what?"

"Like what happened in room 13." Despite himself, Neil smiled a bit. This was good. He and his sister might not be taking after Mom and Dad after all.

"So you're saying that thing we saw was a ghost?" said Bree, crossing her arms. "And that this *ghost* somehow drained the batteries from the flashlight and the camera? To do what?"

"Show herself to us." Neil nodded. Bree simply stood there, her chest heaving. He knew that she was freaking out — especially since she wasn't *talking* about freaking out.

"That's an interesting theory," Bree said. *Exactly. Totally freaked*, Neil thought. "I-I'm tired. I'll see you in the morning. We'll replace those batteries. See what we can find."

Bree closed his door, leaving Neil alone. He slipped under his covers and stared at the ceiling. He briefly wondered how his mother was doing at that moment, down in New Jersey. Then he closed his eyes and tried to shake her face out of his head. Instead, he thought of the ghost: his wonderfully disturbing new distraction. Why would Nurse Janet want to show herself to him? Why had she appeared to Aunt Claire down by the water's edge? And most important, he wondered, had his camera picked up her image before she'd sucked the batteries dry?

Neil turned off the lamp next to his bed. The suburban street lights back home always seeped through his curtains, providing a calming sense of the world outside. Here, the room disappeared into the dead blackness of the countryside night. After a few seconds, his vision adjusted and he made out small details: knobby wooden posts at the end of his bed; the outline of the tall, thin windows; his own skinny hand in front of his face.

Closing his eyes again, sinking into the soft down pillow, Neil's brain buzzed to see the contents of the camera's memory, but when he imagined what — besides Nurse Janet — might be represented there, a strange sensation teased him, as if Graylock's shadows had followed him home, nipping at his heels.

Just before sleep took him away, new questions arose in his mind. Would the asylum in the woods be a salvation, a new kind of hideaway from his troubles? Or was it a trap, pinning him to the darkness of his shadow self?

What was it worth to learn the answer?

CHAPTER
TWELVE

THAT NIGHT, NEIL DREAMED OF THE HOSPITAL.

He was in the back of a van. He couldn't move. Glancing down at his body, he realized he was strapped to a wheelchair. When the vehicle abruptly stopped, someone opened the door, and someone else guided the chair down a wooden ramp to a paved road in the middle of a dense wood. He tried to turn his head, to look around, but his spine was locked down too, tied tightly to a high metallic spindle. Forced to face forward, he saw the road led straight toward a familiar island.

The chain-link fence was gone. The concrete bridge was in perfect shape. Crossing the water, he noticed that the surface was clear of green scum. The healthy reeds grew with an almost culti-vated appearance trim, straight, clean.

Ahead, Graylock Hall waited with a blank expression. If places were capable of thought, this building cared about nothing. It knew it would have him eventually. The boy in the chair was simply another meal, one more soul to sit in a waiting room that would never be full.

He was inside. Tiled walls rushed by. Fast, then faster, until the journey was indistinguishable from a roller-coaster ride. Space Mountain. *Star Wars*. Light speed. Neil wanted to scream, but he realized that his mouth had been clamped shut; leather straps wrapped his skull from crown to jaw.

The chair finally came to a stop in front of a closed door. Green paint flecked off its metal surface. From inside the room, he could hear someone crying. Weeping. Emitting great, gasping sighs. He squeezed his eyes shut, not wanting to see who was in there. But even through his eyelids, he watched the door swing slowly open. Someone pushed the chair into the room, then slammed the door closed with a *whoom!*

Through a high window, clouded daylight fell, illuminating the center of the small room but leaving its corners in shadow. The walls, the ceiling, and the floor were all dingy, puffy, and padded, once white. Flicking his eyes back and forth, Neil noticed long scrapes in the old pads where patients had clawed at the walls, trying to escape. Dark brown streaks painted the edges of the gouged fabric. He imagined broken fingernails, dried blood that no one had ever bothered to clean up. Then, from a shadowed corner, something moved. A voice cried out. No words. A sigh of frustration. A sob of misery. Hopelessness.

The light shifted. Someone was sitting there in the darkness, as if in her own mess, huddled, head down. Dressed in white. A coat with abnormally long sleeves pinned the person's arms to her torso. Stringy, long hair covered her face, draped almost to the floor. Her shoulders shuddered.

Neil grunted, and the person froze, as if suddenly aware of his presence. The figure raised her head, peering at him from behind the wild tangle of hair. She gasped, leaned back against the padded wall, struggled to stand. Then she stumbled forward, barefoot, step step step step, all the way to his wheelchair, threatening to fall face-first into Neil's chest. He pressed himself into his seat, unable to move, unable to cry out.

The person froze, examined him closely, sniffing at his face, his restraints. With the figure directly before him, Neil expected to smell rot, filth, stale breath. Instead, he experienced a recognizable aroma, not unpleasant: roses.

His mother's perfume.

A lightning bolt of nausea melted his muscles.

The woman shook her hair from her face. Though the eyes that peered at him were puffy and red from weeping, they were instantly recognizable, even this desperate and wildly ecstatic.

"Honey," whispered his mother. "Neil, baby. You've got to get us out of here."

But how? he thought.

As if to answer him, she opened her mouth. A purple tongue lolled out, dripping noxious black liquid. This was no longer his mother's face.

She leaned in, as if to kiss him, but at the last second, her cracked lips parted, showing him black gums and several clusters of long, sharp teeth. The brightest white in the darkness.

Neil awoke with a start, and when he did not recognize the room, he cried out quietly.

A moment later, his brain clicked everything into place again. He was at his aunts' house. He'd had a nightmare. A bad one. He let it slip away, but several pieces stuck. The padded room. The figure in the corner. His mother's plea. The horrible face. He took a deep breath, wishing for the glass of water he always remembered to keep next to his bed back home.

He froze, suddenly aware that he wasn't alone.

Someone was crying. Here in his room. The faint sound seemed to have followed him out from the dream. But he wasn't dreaming. In the darkness, he could make out a slumped figure sitting at the end of the bed. She wore a white nightgown. Long brown hair trailed down her back. Her hands were at her face, muffling her soft sobs.

"Bree," Neil said. "What's the matter?"

She flinched at the sound of his voice, then turned to look at him. Her face was in shadow, but he felt her piercing stare, as if she couldn't believe he could actually see her here in the darkness.

"Did you have a bad dream too?" He leaned forward to touch her shoulder, but she stood. Watching him, she backed toward the bedroom door, where she paused before slipping away. She was gone before Neil even had a chance to think of turning on the bedside lamp.

He threw back his sheets and slowly edged toward the door. Near the end of the bed, his bare feet slid on a slick patch of floor. The wood there was wet. "What the . . . ?" He imagined a pool of tears. Had his sister been crying so hard for so long? Was that even possible? Neil bent down. His fingers tingled as the cold moisture clung to his skin. Definitely water. Clutching the mattress to pull himself back up, he realized that his bed was also damp. Had Bree just taken a bath or something? It felt like the middle of the night, but he couldn't say for sure — the clock at his bedside had apparently run out of batteries.

Neil found his way to the hall. He knocked on his sister's door. There was no answer. He turned the knob, pressing his mouth to the crack. "Bree," he whispered. From inside came a soft groan. Neil pushed the door open and stepped in.

Bree was sprawled across the mattress, her sheets and limbs tangled together. She lifted her head from the pillow. "Neil?" she said, her voice foggy with sleep. "What are you doing?"

Neil felt a chill. His shin suddenly pinched at him. "I just came to see if you were okay."

"I'm fine. I was sleeping."

"Sleep*walking* you mean?"

Bree propped herself up on her elbows to see him more clearly. She reached over and turned on her lamp. The room filled with a cozy glow. "Sleepwalking? I don't think so."

Neil flinched. "You were sitting on the edge of my bed. You were crying so hard the floor was wet."

"You were dreaming," said Bree, sounding annoyed.

"I swear I wasn't," he answered. "I'd bet my . . ."

Then he noticed something odd. Bree was wearing a purple T-shirt and gym shorts. Definitely not the white nightgown she'd had on in his bedroom. That chill enveloped him again. He wiped new dampness from his clammy palms onto his pajama pants.

"You'd bet your what?" said Bree.

He was going to say *life*, and was glad he'd stopped himself. It was a bet he would have lost. Moving toward Bree's bed, he pointed to a dark spot on her sheets. "What's this?"

Bree sat up. She touched the stain. "Ew. It's damp."

"I found the same thing in my room," Neil said.

Bree bit her lip. "You swear you're not screwing with me?"

"No way," said Neil. "She was here."

"*Who* was here?"

Neil had a pretty good idea. But he couldn't bring himself to say her name out loud, as if that would draw her back again.

Instead, he explained exactly what had happened to him when he'd woken from his nightmare.

Bree hopped out of bed and stood next to Neil, as if this new closeness would protect them from their fear. "What do we do?" Bree asked.

"Tell the aunts?"

"And freak them out too?"

"Maybe it was one of them?"

"Claire or Anna snuck into both of our rooms and sat on our beds, soaking wet, crying her eyes out." Bree shook her head. "You really believe that?"

"No . . . but what's the other option?" Neil could think of several, none of which provided him with any comfort. Bree must have felt the same way, because she did not answer.

CHAPTER
THIRTEEN

NEIL HAD HEARD STORIES ABOUT PEOPLE who suffered from insomnia, the inability to fall asleep despite a feeling of extreme exhaustion. The morning after the nightmare, he knew exactly how those people felt: horrible. Sitting at the kitchen table, his eyes burned. His scalp hurt, as if every follicle in his head was angry with him. It was cruel, but knowing that Bree was experiencing the same thing made Neil feel a bit better. She sat across from him, leaning on the table, propping her head on her crossed arms.

The night before, she'd come back to his room with him. They'd kept the light on, lying restlessly on his bed until early morning light spilled through the windows. The aunts found the two of them a couple hours later sprawled half-conscious on the couch downstairs, the television blaring an obnoxious aerobics program.

The incident with the visitor accounted for only part of Neil's sleep-depriving anxiety; mostly, he was afraid that if he allowed himself to fall fully asleep, he'd return to that padded cell in the dream asylum, where the purple-tongued demoness was waiting to finish her meal.

"So the beds are uncomfortable," Anna said, placing the carton of orange juice in the center of the table.

"No, no." Bree shook her head. "They're *really* comfortable."

Claire and Anna glanced at each other. "Then why were you two down here?" Anna asked. The silence that followed was as sharp as a knife.

Why couldn't he just spit it out? Finally, Neil decided he *could*. After all, maybe the aunts had answers. "Actually," he said, "someone came into our rooms last night. It sort of freaked us out."

Again, a glance between the aunts; this one, however, was of confusion. And it revealed the answer to a question he hadn't even asked. *It wasn't either of us*, it said.

"Someone?" said Claire.

"She had long brown hair," said Neil. "Dressed in what I thought was a white nightgown. But it might have been something else. A uniform maybe."

"And you both saw her?" Anna asked.

Bree lifted her head. "Well . . . no. But there was a puddle on my floor."

Anna scowled. "Neil. Please. Your sister doesn't need you playing jokes on her like this."

Neil's face flushed. "It's not like that." He glanced at Bree for help, but she was looking at him as if considering that Anna might be onto something. "We think the woman might have been . . . well, a ghost."

Now Anna glared at Claire. "All that talk about Graylock yesterday," she murmured.

Claire sat down at the table. She reached out and took both of their hands. "You guys," she said, "I want you to *talk* to us if you're feeling upset or . . . strange about everything that's been going on back home. Anna and I understand this is a really difficult time for you. For your mom. And your dad."

Neil grunted. No one seemed to notice. He chewed on the inside of his lip, annoyed. He'd worked up the courage to tell them what was really happening. Why did Claire have to change the subject?

"Thanks," said Bree. "We know it's hard for you too. Having us here."

"But what about the possibility of a ghost?" Neil interrupted. Slowly, everyone turned to look at him. "You told us about what you saw at Graylock Lake, Aunt Claire. The woman in the reeds. What if that was Nurse Janet? What if she followed . . . I mean, maybe the person we saw last night was her too?"

"Nurse Janet?" said Claire unsurely.

Anna snorted and shook her head. "She's a boogeywoman. A ghost story someone made up to keep kids in line."

"I heard she worked at that hospital," Neil persisted. "They say she still haunts it. That she drowns kids who break into Graylock Hall. She kills them just like she killed her patients when she was still alive."

"*Neil!*" Bree said through her teeth.

"If that's true," said Anna, squinting at him, "whatever was she doing *here* last night? According to you, Neil, she comes after kids who break into Graylock, right?"

Claire stood up. "Okay. All right. Enough ghost talk. We don't want anyone having bad dreams again tonight."

"It wasn't a bad dream," said Neil, right before remembering the extremely bad dream that had woken him up in the first place.

"I don't care if it was acid indigestion," said Anna. "The Nurse Janet story is a lie that was started by parents who had good, if not slightly warped, intentions: to keep the doors of that creepy build-ing locked tight. No one should be going in there. Not anymore."

Neil pressed his lips together. *You've got to get us out of here*, his mother had insisted in the dream from the night before. If learn-ing the truth about Nurse Janet could prove that she had come to him, that he hadn't *imagined* it — that he wasn't taking after his mom — then he didn't care what building he had to sneak into.

No one would stop him.

CHAPTER
FOURTEEN

AFTER BREAKFAST, BREE DECIDED TO STAY BEHIND and help Anna out in her ceramics studio, which was tucked discreetly inside the ramshackle barn that stood behind the aunts' house.

Claire insisted that Neil accompany her to the pie shop, where she assured him that she would reveal all of her baking secrets. Neil had no choice but to follow, even though he couldn't have cared less about the *secret of pie*. Before they got in the car, he grabbed the satchel from the chair next to his bed, wondering when he'd have the opportunity to hunt for haunts.

As they pulled out of the driveway, Neil half-expected to see Nurse Janet standing with a wide grin at the side of the road, her thumb extended to hitch a ride. He closed his eyes until they were nearly at the shop, which was already bustling with Claire's employees.

In the kitchen, Claire introduced Neil to the head pastry chef, Glenn Kelly, a tall and surprisingly skinny man with a big smile who wore a pristine white apron over a white T-shirt and jeans. His assistant was a college-age girl named Melissa Diaz, also thin with wide hips and a chest Neil knew he should not be staring at. She apparently couldn't be bothered to glance at Neil for more than three seconds. Manning the register in the shop itself was a thick-necked high school boy, Lyle Peters, whose eyes were still puffy with sleep. When Claire approached the shop's front doors to unbolt the locks, a small crowd swooshed in, money in hand.

Neil lounged in one of the booths, wishing he could leave, but Claire had told him she didn't want him wandering off alone, glancing at his bandaged leg as she said it. The longer he sat there by himself, the easier it was for his parents to creep back inside his head. As strange as it sounded, he'd rather be visited by the weeping woman from the night before than to dream of his mother in the padded cell ever again.

"Hey, Neil," a voice called from the back of the shop. Melissa stood in the kitchen doorway. "We need some help with this crust. Get off your butt."

Neil wasn't sure whether to smile or scowl. Claire stood behind the cash register, pointedly ignoring him. He followed Melissa as she turned away, unsure of what he was getting himself into.

A couple hours later, Neil was covered with flour and proud of it. He'd rolled out at least twenty crusts and pinched them into single pie plates. Glenn had complimented him on his technique, and eventually Melissa had to admit that, at the very least, he was a fast learner.

"What happened to your leg?" Melissa asked him when Glenn was out of earshot. "Looks serious."

"Oh, this?" Neil glanced at his bandage. "I was out at . . ." Whoops. He'd almost just told this girl what had actually happened. He had to be careful. Her appearance was distracting.

"You were out at, what?"

"The woods. I tripped over a log."

Melissa laughed, then covered her mouth. "I'm sorry. A log?" She became mock-serious. "Are you a klutz? Should I be worried about having you here in the kitchen?"

"No. I'm not a klutz." Neil could feel his face turning red. "I just didn't see it there."

"So what you're saying is: The log attacked you."

Neil pressed his lips together. He knew she was just teasing him. Still . . . "Actually, I fell through the floor out at Graylock Hall," he blurted out.

"Graylock?" Melissa flinched. Instead of being mock-serious, she now looked truly serious. Maybe even a little frightened.

"I went yesterday with my sister and some friends." And now for the clincher. "We snuck in through a window."

"What were you thinking? And who are these friends? I thought you weren't from here."

"Wesley and Eric Baptiste." He regretted saying their names immediately. What if Melissa told on them?

"Really?" Melissa softened. "Eric went with you?"

"You know him?"

Melissa nodded. "He's in my little brother's band. We actually went out a couple years ago. I was a senior. He was a sophomore. He's pretty cute."

Neil didn't know what to say. The best he could think of was: "I'm pretty sure my sister would agree with you."

"Well, tell your sister to stay away from him if she values her sanity," said Melissa, turning back to the pie crusts.

Oh, Neil thought, *she does. We both do.*

"Trust me," Melissa added. "Cute does not always mean sweet."

"I think Bree figured that out already."

"Neil!" Claire popped her head through the doorway and called out through the din, "You've got a visitor."

Neil leaned close to Melissa. "Don't tell anyone what I told you. You know, about Graylock?"

Melissa raised an eyebrow. "Why not?"

"I don't want to get anyone in trouble. Please?"

Melissa smiled. "You know the best way to keep a secret?" Neil shook his head. "Never tell anyone. Period."

Carrying his satchel, Neil wandered out to the café section of the shop. He found Wesley standing just inside the front door, sweating through his bright orange tie-dyed T-shirt. Claire had given him a cup of water. Outside, Neil saw Wesley's bike propped against the café's large front window.

The events of the previous day careened back into Neil's brain, and he realized that the pie shop had so consumed him, he hadn't even thought about the nighttime visitor since Melissa had asked him to help with the crusts.

"Hey there!" said Wesley. "I called your house. Your sister told me you were here."

"Cool," said Neil. "I'm glad you came."

"She said you had something to tell me." Wesley clasped the water cup tightly, looking as if he expected to hear a mind-blowing story.

"I sure do." Neil called out to his aunt, who was behind the counter chatting with Lyle. "Aunt Claire, can I take a break?"

"Hmm," Claire said, glancing up. When she saw Wesley, she smiled. "You're going together, right?"

"Just to the playground," said Wesley. "Over on Bennett Street."

"Don't be too long."

"We won't," said Neil, already reaching for the doorknob.

CHAPTER
FIFTEEN

As they walked several blocks toward Bennett Street — passing quiet houses and overgrown gardens, ramshackle fences and cars in gravel driveways that looked as if they'd been abandoned — Neil told Wesley what had happened the night before.

Wesley nearly fell down with excitement. "Nurse Janet totally followed you home!"

"I'm not sure that's something to cheer about," said Neil. "Doesn't the legend say that she looks for new victims to drown?"

Wesley grew somber. "Oh yeah. I forgot about that part."

At Bennett, they took a left and encountered a large field. The playground stood at the crest of a nearby hill. Once they'd reached the blanket of green grass, they began to climb.

"Shoot," said Neil. "I still don't have camera batteries. I wanted to check out the pictures from yesterday."

"What kind of batteries do you need?" asked Wesley, racing toward the empty swing set at the top of the slope.

"Not sure," said Neil, trying to keep up. "Double A?"

When they reached the playground, Wesley leapt into the seat of a swing. His momentum carried him swiftly backward and up. Grasping a chain with one hand, he reached into his pocket with the other. When he swung back toward Neil, he showed him what he'd brought — two small cylinders marked AA. "Will these work?"

Neil smiled and then jumped back so that Wesley wouldn't kick him in the chest. "Those will totally work."

"You can thank Bree. She was the one who reminded me. I pulled them out of our TV remote. Should still have some juice left. Here. Catch."

Neil sat on the still swing beside Wesley and carefully opened the slot in the side of the camera. After replacing the old batteries with the newish ones, Neil took a deep breath and then pressed the POWER button. A second later, the lens whirred open as the view screen blinked on. "Yes!" said Neil. "Thank you, Wesley!"

Wesley dropped his feet to the worn-out ground and skidded to a stop. "So . . . what'd you get?"

Neil hit the REVIEW button, and an image popped up on the screen: a brightly lit doorknob. This was the last picture. Room 13. "Wait," he said. "Let's start from the beginning." He selected the slide show function, and suddenly the two boys were watching a recap of the previous day's misadventure, filmstrip style.

The first few pictures showed the front of the hospital — the circular drive, the ivy, the solid main-entrance doors. The sky was blue. The light was golden. The shots revealed nothing about the secrets locked inside. In fact, the place looked almost pretty.

Next, the camera showed the gymnasium — the warped floorboards, the decaying ceiling. This was more like it. Still, Neil saw nothing that might be paranormal. No mists. No floating orbs. No shadows filled with faces. The only faces that appeared were in the group shot of Wesley, Bree, and Eric huddled together underneath one of the basketball hoops.

They journeyed up the dark stairs to the labyrinth of hallways. Chipped tiles. Dusty gurneys. Toppled wheelchairs. There was one particularly disturbing picture of a large black spider, but no ghosts. Not yet.

The youth ward appeared with its giant, sunlit windows. There were pictures of the cake table, the rack of stuffed animals. In one shot of the stairwell, a small bulb of light hovered near the top of the screen, but Neil could not be certain whether or not it was merely a speck of dust. That was the problem with orbs — according to Alexi and Mark, they were very inconsistent phenomena.

Then the camera showed them the doorknob picture again, shiny, bluish-white. Overexposed. They'd reached the end. Neil felt faint with annoyance.

"That's it?" said Wesley, standing. "No ghosts. Are you sure you guys didn't just imagine seeing something in the room with you?" He began to pace in front of the swing set.

"I *thought* I was sure," said Neil. "But maybe we were wrong."

A light flickered at his hand. Neil glanced back at the camera. The slide show had progressed. On the screen, a new image stared up at them: a taxidermic deer head hanging on a wood panel wall, wide antlers reaching toward a soot-stained ceiling. "What the heck?" said Neil. He didn't remember taking this picture.

Wesley stared at him from the far swing, looking concerned.

The slide show continued on. The next shot revealed what appeared to be a piano bench. A stack of sheet music stood precariously on the edge, ready to topple. The top sheet read *Superstition, music by Stevie Wonder.* In another picture was a fireplace. Three decorative birch logs were arranged just so upon a set of plain andirons.

"What is it?" Wesley asked, rushing back. But by the time he reached Neil's shoulder, the screen had turned blue. The slide show was over. Neil stared at the camera for several seconds. Then he quickly told Wesley what he'd seen.

"You're sure those shots aren't from your aunts' house? Maybe someone took them last night after you got home."

"I'm positive," said Neil, feeling queasy. "And besides, the camera wasn't working last night. Remember?"

"Let me see."

Neil scrolled quickly through the pictures. The catalogue of Graylock photographs appeared, but the last three, the ones Neil didn't remember taking, were now missing.

"They were right here," said Neil, totally confused.

The screen went black. A gust of wind rustled the grass all the way down the hill. Neil clutched the camera tightly. He felt a hand against the small of his back. He turned to look at Wesley, who clearly was not touching him. Neil felt pressure between his shoulder blades. His sneakers dragged forward as the swing began to move. Neil turned his head to see who was pushing him.

No one was there.

Neil leapt off the seat and ran from the swing set. The swing beside Wesley moved back and forth. Back and forth. Back and forth. As if someone had taken his place. Then the swing suddenly stopped, the chains hung straight down. Neil almost fell backward, but caught himself just in time. "Someone pushed me," he said. Wesley stared at the seat in astonishment.

For some reason, Neil turned and glanced down the hill. In the middle of the street, a hundred yards away, a figure was watching him. She was dressed in white. He held his hand above his eyes to shield the sun, but he couldn't make out her face.

Fingers clutched his wrist, and Neil shrieked. It was Wesley. Wesley laughed and then asked, "What are you looking at?"

"That woman . . ." Neil pointed. But the street was empty. His skin felt as if it had been replaced by sandpaper. He was itchy all over.

"What woman?" Wesley stepped forward. "Neil? You're acting weird."

"She was right there! Don't tell me I was the only one who saw her."

"Sorry."

Neil didn't want to hear anymore. He tossed the camera back into the satchel. "I'm not imagining things. Let's go find her."

The boys explored every alley on the way back, but they found no woman wearing a white uniform.

When they burst through the shop's front doors, several customers looked up at them. Neil realized that his chest was heaving and his eyes were wide. He slipped into the booth near the front door, where he put his head in his hands, trying impossibly to hide. He couldn't come in here acting like a total freak, but that's exactly how he felt. Even Wesley "Green Man" Baptiste was looking at him funny.

He'd hoped that seeing the ghost again would take him away from everything of which he was frightened. Now he was worried that he was seeing things: first the phantom photos in the camera and then the woman in the street. *You've got to get us out of here*, his dream mother had said. But, it seemed, Neil had only traveled farther into the padded room.

Claire waved at the boys as the café's phone rang. She picked it up. Thankfully, she hadn't noticed their dramatic entrance.

"What do we do?" Wesley whispered.

"We have to tell Bree," said Neil.

"Eric too," said Wesley. "Maybe they'll have an idea about those extra pictures. Try the camera again."

Neil pulled the device out from the bag, but the screen wouldn't change from black no matter how many times he hit the POWER button. He shook his head, disappointed. Dead batteries — again! This had to mean the woman he'd seen in the street had been a spirit, didn't it? He clicked open the camera's small side panel, slid the batteries out, and handed them back to Wesley.

"You don't think I'm crazy, do you?" he asked.

Before Wesley could answer, Claire approached and slid into the booth next to him. "*So!*" she said. "It turns out we're having a party tonight. And guess what?"

"What?" the boys asked at the same time.

"You're both invited."

CHAPTER
SIXTEEN

EVERY MONTH, THE AUNTS AND THEIR FRIENDS GOT TOGETHER to drink and eat and watch their favorite "Best Bad Movies." With the arrival of their niece and nephew that week, Claire and Anna had forgotten that the movie night was upon them. And worse, it was their turn to host. A group of at least eight adults would be showing up around seven thirty that evening, expecting hors d'oeuvres.

After a stop at the grocery store, Neil felt a chill as he walked through the aunts' front door. He wasn't sure if he was ready to meet their friends. What if they asked him why he was staying in Hedston for the summer?

Claire followed Neil into the house, calling out, "Anna, turn on the oven! We found some frozen snacks."

Anna peeked her head out from the kitchen. "Frozen?" She screwed up her face.

Neil stood at the bottom of the foyer staircase, holding a paper grocery bag. His cheeks burned with embarrassment. "Easy there," said Claire, lugging the rest of the load down the hall. "Neil picked out the menu. And I have complete trust in him." He couldn't help but smile at that. Claire was actually pretty cool. He decided then that he needed to start giving her more of a chance.

A *bang* sounded upstairs, followed by a frightened scream.

Neil grabbed the banister, steadying himself. Claire and Anna raced from the kitchen, looking up at the ceiling.

"Bree?" Claire called. "Everything okay?"

Bree careened to the top of the staircase and dashed halfway down before realizing that everyone was there staring at her. "I — I," she stammered, trembling, unable to continue.

Anna raced to the bottom of the steps, nearly knocking Neil out of the way. She climbed the stairs, meeting Bree where she stood. She grabbed her shoulders and gave a brief hug. "Honey," she said calmly, "what's wrong?"

Bree took a deep breath. "I was in the bathroom. I lifted the toilet seat." Neil wasn't sure he wanted to hear the rest of this. "And inside . . ." Bree shuddered. "Snakes!"

That was *not* what Neil was expecting her to say.

"Oh my god," said Claire.

"Like, tons and tons of long green snakes!" Bree seemed to become aware of herself. She held her palms in front of her face, rubbing at her eyes. "I'm sorry. I'm acting like a kid."

Anna steadied herself, glancing up the stairs with shoulders squared, as if she had to deal with this kind of thing every day.

"I'm not going back in there," said Bree, wriggling away from Anna, descending the rest of the steps to stand by Neil. But now Neil was curious.

"I'll go," he said, following Anna up the stairs.

Bree had managed to close the bathroom door in her desperate scramble to escape the alleged toilet snakes. Anna and Neil stood in the hallway, staring at the knob, worried together what might happen when they pushed the door open. Would a mass of wriggling green serpents spill forth, mouths open wide, fangs dripping with venom, ready to chomp their ankles? Would they make a good snake-stomping duo? Anna certainly looked as if she was ready to destroy something. She pressed her ear to the door, then shook her head. "I don't hear anything." She glanced at Neil. "Feeling brave, kiddo?"

Neil nodded, even though he wasn't sure. He reached out, turned the knob, and pushed.

A lightbulb glowed dimly from the ceiling above, Bree obviously having forgotten to turn it off. The toilet sat beside a purple porcelain claw-foot bathtub. Of course, the lid was down.

Anna crept forward, reaching for the bowl scrubber perched just behind the pipes next to the tub. A weapon. Neil stayed behind her now, happy that Anna had decided to become the brave one here. He heard a rustling sound from the hall, and he turned to find Claire watching from just outside the door. Standing several feet from the toilet, Anna used the scrubber handle as a prop, slowly raising both the lid and the seat. They clinked against the water tank behind the bowl.

From where he stood, Neil could not see over the lip. He looked at Anna's face to get a clue what was inside. She looked disgusted and confused, but not afraid.

"What the . . . ," Anna whispered. Stepping closer, she used the scrubber to reach inside the bowl. When she lifted it, tentatively, slowly, something long, green, and slightly fuzzy hung from the scrubber's plastic bristles. "Lake weed."

"How the heck did *that* get in there?" said Claire, stepping into the bathroom.

Neil's mouth went dry. He clenched his fingers against his palms, trying to stop them from going numb. He leaned forward to get a better view. He needed to see exactly what his sister had seen.

The toilet bowl was filled with long strands of the noxious-looking grass bunched up in clumps. They looked almost alive in the water, serpent-like.

The weed was the same type he'd seen one day earlier, swirling just below the surface of the lake out by Graylock Hall.

CHAPTER
SEVENTEEN

"STRANGE THINGS HAPPEN OUT HERE IN THE COUNTRY," said Anna, arranging small quiches on a baking tray next to the open oven door. Neil and Bree worked near the sink, mixing a packet of ranch dip with a carton of sour cream. "A long time ago, when I told my family I was moving to New York City from Nowheresville, Pennsylvania, they asked me if I was scared. I guess I was, but the city is a particular kind of scary, where you have several simple rules to stay safe. Watch your back. Be aware of your surroundings. Don't ride the subway alone late at night. I even carried around a can of pepper spray, which thankfully, I never used.

"When I left New York to move up here with Claire, my friends had the same reaction that my family'd had when I'd gone to the city: *Are you scared?*" Anna slid the tray into the oven and closed the door. "To be honest, I find the country to be much more frightening. Up here, you never know what you're going to get, so it's nearly impossible to prepare the way you can in the city. Mysterious sounds in the woods at night. Strange lights in the sky."

"Lake weed in the pipes," said Bree, blushing again. She'd cleaned the stringy grass out of the toilet bowl herself, embarrassed that she'd caused such a scene.

"And no one can hear you scream," said Claire in a low, dramatic voice. She opened a cupboard and pulled down a stack of

mismatched china plates. "I know people who are scared by the sound of nighttime crickets." She laughed. "We got used to it fairly quickly. You find ways to feel less alone. Mostly by maintaining the few friendships you have . . . by getting together with people who understand you."

"Seems to me that you guys have plenty of friends," said Bree, popping a piece of celery into her mouth.

"Speaking of which," Anna said, glancing at the clock above the refrigerator, "those friends will be here soon. Television's working, right?"

"It was working this morning," said Bree.

"That's right!" said Claire. "Are you two planning on getting up at the crack of dawn again tomorrow?"

Neil blinked, thinking to himself, *Hopefully, we won't have a reason to.* He watched his sister out of the corner of his eye — she wore a blank smile, appearing to have recovered entirely from The Great Toilet Snake Incident. He wondered if she'd be so cool when he and Wesley told her everything that had happened that day.

The doorbell rang. The first of the guests had arrived. Others quickly followed. Neil recognized a few of them from the pie shop. Soon, a small din rose from the living room, where the adults sat and ate and drank and laughed. Claire and Anna introduced Neil and Bree to everyone, and thankfully, no one asked about their mother or father. The guests all seemed genuinely pleased to meet them. There was a young couple, Barry and Libba, who had driven forty-five minutes from outside of Albany; an older woman, Gladys, whose black dress was covered with white cat hair; a few other shop owners from downtown Hedston; a quiet man, named Olivier, who sometimes helped Anna in her studio.

Last but not least was Andy — the man who had come upon the battered, bloody group the day before. Today he was dressed in a black polo shirt, dark jeans, and work boots — cleaned up from the plaid-shirted, woodsman look he'd worn when they met him. He smiled mischievously at Neil and Bree when they realized why they recognized him.

"How's that leg feeling?" Andy asked.

"It's better," said Neil, his heart racing. He didn't feel like telling the story of his injury to this group of strangers. But Andy was kind enough to drop it.

"What movie are you all watching?" Bree asked, boldly sitting beside Gladys, risking a staticky cat-hair transfer.

"Aren't you going to watch it too?" Gladys asked.

"Depends on what it is."

"It's the hosts' choice," said Andy, waving for Claire and Anna to answer.

Sitting on the arm of the couch, Claire turned toward Bree. "We have some ground rules. This is 'Best Bad Movie Night,' remember. The film has to be campy, trashy, scary, over-the-top. It has to be at least as old as any of us. We try to weed out anything *too* gory or nasty."

"Sometimes unsuccessfully," said Andy, laughing.

"All that being said," Claire continued, "I've pulled a classic from our personal catalogue that, for some reason, this group has not experienced together." Everyone leaned forward, as if Claire was about to spill a life-changing secret. "*Whatever Happened to Baby Jane?*"

The room filled with oohs and aahs. And a couple groans.

"Now, now," said Gladys. "Hosts get final say."

"We didn't have a lot of time to plan," Anna muttered, almost to herself.

"I've never heard of it," said Neil.

"Never heard of *Baby Jane*?" Anna's mouth dropped open. She continued excitedly, "Bette Davis plays a psychotic former child actress who locks up her paralyzed sister, played by Joan Crawford, in a decaying Hollywood mansion." When Neil and Bree stared back, blankly, she went on, "Oh, come on! You must have seen the dead-rat-on-a-dinner-plate scene somewhere on the Internet. What else is YouTube good for but silly little things like that?"

"Stop, Anna! You'll spoil it for them!" said Claire.

Dead rats on dinner plates? Neil cringed. The word *psychotic* made him nervous.

"Are you convinced to watch with us now, Bree?" said Gladys, smirking.

There was a knock at the door. Wesley! Finally. Neil leapt up from his chair. "I'll get it."

When Neil opened the door, he was surprised to find Eric standing beside his brother. "Hey, Neil," Eric said. "Looking good. Better than last time I saw you."

Wesley looked a little embarrassed. "He borrowed Mom's car to drive me. Is it all right if he stays?"

Neil glanced into the living room. Bree's antennae were up. She craned her neck to see who he was talking to. Neil forced a smile. "Sure," he said to the brothers. "Come on in."

CHAPTER
EIGHTEEN

NEIL LED WESLEY AND ERIC INTO THE KITCHEN, offering them something to drink. Curious, Bree snuck in behind them.

Accepting a glass of Coke from Neil, Eric glanced into the living room. "This is weird," he said, then took a swig.

"I can get you something else instead," said Neil.

"Not the Coke," said Eric. "Them." He nodded at the small group of adults. "What are they all doing here?"

"Having fun," said Bree, crossing her arms. "What are *you* doing here?"

Wesley took a step toward Neil, as if bracing himself for an explosion.

Eric frowned. Placing the glass on the counter, he said, "I'm sorry. Did I do something to you?"

Bree shrugged. "Besides leaving us alone in an abandoned mental hospital?"

"I didn't leave you alone."

"You went off by yourself. Neil got hurt. We're lucky it wasn't worse."

"You're right," said Eric. "It *could* have been worse. But it wasn't. So what's your problem?"

"I don't understand why you'd come to someone's house for a party and then call everyone weird. That's all. Maybe this is why your band kicked you out? You seem a little bit . . . insensitive."

"They didn't kick me out," Eric said, exasperated. "I *quit*."

"Guys!" said Neil, waving them quiet.

But Eric went on, "To answer your question, Wesley asked me to come inside. That's why I'm here. I wasn't planning on staying."

Wesley finally spoke up. "We need to talk. All of us. Together."

Bree and Eric paused, and then looked at Wesley as if he'd poked them with a stick.

"Something happened today," said Neil nervously. "Something really weird." He told Eric about the ghostly visitor the night before, about the puddle of water at the end of his and Bree's beds. He explained that an invisible hand had pushed him on the playground swing, that a woman dressed in white had vanished while watching them from Bennett Street. He described the pictures that had disappeared from the camera, and the weeds that had come through the pipes into the upstairs bathroom.

When Neil was done, an uncomfortable silence hung in the kitchen. "What if something happened when we went to Graylock yesterday?" Neil added, lowering his voice. "Is it crazy to think that whatever appeared in room 13 followed us home?"

"Nurse Janet?" said Eric, as if considering the possibility for the first time.

"I can't stop thinking about the legend," said Neil. "That her ghost drowns kids out in the lake." Bree held her hand up to her mouth. Eric dropped the cocky mask he'd worn since he'd arrived. They both looked truly frightened.

Neil felt oddly pleased with their reaction. At the very least, it made his theory seem reasonable.

"You think she's toying with you?" asked Eric.

Neil's pleasure was brief. If they were being haunted, then he wasn't imagining things; however, Nurse Janet wasn't exactly the kind of spirit Neil wanted lurking around his bedroom late at night.

"There's got to be something we can do to stop her," said Wesley.

"Oh really?" said Bree. "How exactly do we stop a ghost?"

"A ghost?" said a voice from the doorway. "How exciting!" The four of them spun around. Gladys, the cat-hair lady, stood there smiling at them, holding an empty wine glass. "I'm sorry! I didn't mean to scare you." She took up the bottle from the kitchen table. "Oh, your aunts wanted me to tell you that they're starting the movie." Looking directly into Neil's eyes, she said, "I think you're going to like this one."

Neil sat on the couch next to Wesley. Halfway through, he was fairly certain that old actress's pale face would haunt his dreams. And that voice! If he ever heard her muttering in the dark of his bedroom, he knew he'd scream to wake the neighbors, no matter how far away they lived out here in the country.

Near the end of the movie, Neil went to the kitchen for a drink and stayed there until it was over. While the adults talked about the film, Wesley came and found him. "Let's take a walk," he whispered. They snuck out the front door with Eric and Bree.

On the porch, Eric stood close to Bree and said, "We need a plan."

"I have a suggestion!" said Bree, feigning excitement. "We could go to the store and just buy some ghost repellant." She dropped her smile and crossed her arms, glaring at Eric.

"I hear it's cheaper if we just order online," he answered with a smirk.

Bree clenched her fists.

"We do have a ghost expert here," said Wesley, stepping between them. "Neil knows what to do. Right, Neil?"

Put on the spot, Neil suddenly felt his throat start to close up. His mind went blank. "I'll check the *Ghostly Investigators'* website. I'm sure they'll have a few good suggestions."

"I have one," said Eric. "First, how about we confirm that we're actually dealing with something supernatural."

Neil flinched. "What do you mean? Ghosts *are* supernatural."

"Yeah. But you're the only one who's seen it. How do we know you're telling the truth?"

"I'm telling the truth," Neil said, unable to keep from sounding annoyed.

"You *think* you are, at least."

The ground started to feel wobbly. Neil grabbed hold of the porch railing.

"Eric!" Wesley whispered, horrified.

"Look," said Bree, stepping closer to Eric. "If my brother says he saw a ghost, he saw a ghost. We didn't ask for your help."

Eric's mouth dropped open. "I didn't mean anything by it. I'm only saying —"

"It doesn't matter what you're saying," said Bree. "Because we're no longer listening."

CHAPTER
NINETEEN

AFTER ERIC AND WESLEY DROVE OFF, Neil sat on the front steps with his sister, taking in the sounds of the night — a totally different experience than in New Jersey. Up here in the Catskills wilderness, the wind through the trees had a voice that wasn't drowned out by the constant drone of engines on the Turnpike. Neil and Bree gazed at the stars, which shined clearly overhead, a burst of fireworks frozen in the night sky. At home, only half as many were visible, hidden behind a red haze that leaked like an algae bloom from the lights of New York City across the Hudson River.

Here, they could see how things were supposed to be.

"Sorry I made your friends leave," said Bree, staring at her feet.

"It's okay. Thanks for sticking up for me."

Bree glanced at him quickly. "I called Mom today."

Neil shuddered, unable to control himself. He smacked at his arms, trying to pass off his reaction as a battle with a mosquito. "She picked up?" he asked, hoping he didn't sound desperate.

"No. But I left a message. I told her that we're thinking about her."

But I'm trying not *to think about her*, Neil thought.

Bree tried to take his hand, but he snatched it away, pretending this time that a mosquito was buzzing near his leg. When he looked, there actually *was* a mosquito buzzing around. Several. Quite a few in fact. "We're gonna get eaten if we stay out here," he said.

They stood and went to the door. Voices came through the screen.

"Shh," said Bree, holding Neil back. They listened.

"Oh, I don't think they thought of the movie that way," said Anna from the living room, her voice hushed. "Stop being such a drama queen, Claire."

"*Okay*," said Claire. "All I'm saying is that next time, maybe we should think a little bit harder about the movies we decide to watch in front of these kids."

"What are they talking about?" Neil whispered.

Bree sighed. "What do you think, dummy? Us."

"I'm sorry," said Gladys, "I don't understand. The Baby Jane character is nothing like Linda. Why would they even be upset?"

"I was just thinking out loud," said Claire. "After what they did yesterday, breaking into that hospital and everything —"

Neil felt his stomach hit the floor. Bree grabbed his arm. *They knew about the trip to Graylock?* Who'd told them? Had it been Andy? Dr. Simon? Melissa Diaz had been the only other person Neil had mentioned it to.

"— and then how they slept last night, or *didn't* sleep . . . Something weird is going on. I can't explain it."

"Something weird?" said Anna. "An understatement, Claire, my dear. Their father's completely out of the picture. Their mother basically kicked them out of her house for the summer. I'm surprised they haven't spontaneously combusted."

"Especially with the two of us tiptoeing around," Claire added. "I've never felt so clueless. I'm beginning to wonder if they wouldn't be better off with my brother in Jersey City."

Neil squeezed his mouth shut, hoping to keep inside the groan he felt bubbling up from his gut.

"Kids are unpredictable," said Andy, his voice even, soothing. "When *my* wife went away, my daughter was a complete wreck. I really have to commend you two for trying to pick up the pieces here."

"I wouldn't put it that way," said Claire. "We love those kids. We just want what's best."

"Neil and Bree seem pretty strong," said Gladys.

Andy chuckled. "I suppose you're right, Glad. That they went exploring Graylock Hall is almost quaint. On the other hand, if they start locking themselves in their rooms, refusing to speak, refusing to eat . . . *then* I would worry." He paused and sighed. "You four will be fine, no matter what happens with Linda. Trust me. I've been there. I know."

Neil tried to pull away from Bree, but when he shifted his weight, the porch creaked. Loudly. The voices inside went quiet. *"Gnats!"* he whispered, squeezing his eyes shut.

"Bree?" Anna called. "Neil?"

Bree took a few silent steps backward, getting as far away from the screen door as possible while remaining on the deck. "We're outside, Aunt Anna!" Then she treaded heavily back to the entry, making it sound as though they'd been far away from the conversation. Neil rolled his eyes, following behind, deciding to just go with it.

But it turned out, once he'd come into the living room, it was as though the conversation hadn't taken place. "Want some ice cream?" asked Claire, all her worries hidden behind her smile, like stars in a light-polluted sky.

CHAPTER
TWENTY

NEIL RAN THROUGH DARKNESS. Someone was chasing him.

He splashed into shallow water, tripped, then fell, reaching out and stopping himself before his face went under. The ground below the water's surface felt slimy, dank, a living kind of muck, as if the earth itself were trying to pull him down. He pulled back.

Standing, he realized that he was knee-deep in the lake. Lily pads swirled around his legs, their long green stalks tangling around his calves.

Rain sprinkled from a slate-black sky. Lightning flashed in the distance, revealing a horizon of sharp pine trees reflected in the lake below. A stone building on the shore shined brightly for a moment before disappearing quickly into the dark cloak of rain and wind. He knew where he was. Graylock. Of course.

Someone barreled through the brush behind him. A white light bounced in the black night air, reflecting harshly off the tall reeds, the water, the pine tree branches high above. The light blinded him.

Neil froze — unable to think, unable to breathe. The muck was sucking on his feet. Whoever held the flashlight shined it directly into his face. He held up his hands, trying to make out who was on the other side of the beam, but all he could see was a bulky, featureless silhouette.

The figure came at him, pushing him backward. Unprepared, Neil tumbled once more into the lake. This time he could not find the bottom. His hands caught in the lake weed. He tried to jerk himself away from it, but the grass seemed to yank back. He tried to pluck the fuzzy strands away, but they tightened, anchoring him to the lake bed. He kicked, struggled to catch air, but he'd gone deeper than he expected.

All around, there was only water.

Water, and the black of the beyond.

He opened his mouth, and darkness filled his lungs.

Neil woke, choking, unable to catch his breath. A sensation of pins and needles pressed every inch of his skin. It hurt so much, he clutched at his sweat-soaked sheets.

Moments later, the feeling abated. His throat opened, and he gasped.

There was a knock at the door. "You okay in there?" Aunt Claire. His restlessness must have woken her too.

He tried to speak, but his voice came out harsh, as if he'd gargled with concrete. "I think I had a bad dream."

Claire pushed the door open. "Are you decent?"

"I hope so," he said, his voice cracking.

She came in and stood at the end of his bed. "I'm sorry," she said. "That stupid movie."

"It wasn't the movie," said Neil.

"I feel guilty," she said, ignoring his comment. "Let me get you some water. I'll stay for a while."

Neil sighed. The room began to feel like a room again instead of a portal to another time and place. "You don't have to do that."

"But I do, and I will," said his aunt, turning to go. "Be right back."

As soon as she said it, Neil was glad. He really didn't want to be alone right now.

In the morning, Claire was gone. Neil crawled groggily out from under his covers. Once again, he stepped into a cool puddle near the end of his bed. The water sent goose bumps from the soles of his feet to the top of his skull.

His dream of the lake came back to him, along with the painful sensation of drowning, and a deeply unsettling thought dawned on him. It hadn't felt like a dream at all — it had felt much more like a memory. A memory of something that had actually happened.

But it wasn't *his* memory. So whose was it?

Neil shook his head in a useless attempt to clear his mind. He dashed downstairs, still in his pajamas, hoping to find the others awake and about.

The aunts were sitting on the front porch, drinking orange juice. A cool morning breeze swept across the front lawn. Honeyed sunlight coated every green thing with a sweet glow. It was bound to be a gorgeous day. Claire and Anna glanced up at him as he pushed open the squeaky screen door. He blinked and said good morning, wiping his damp feet against the wood planks, removing evidence of the ghostly visitor.

"Where's Bree?" Neil asked, sitting in a broken red Adirondack chair that leaned against the porch rail.

"She's using the computer in my studio," said Anna. "Wanted to send some e-mails to her friends back in New Jersey."

"Is it okay if I check my e-mail too?"

"Sure," said Anna. "But give Bree some space. She seemed a little upset this morning."

This sparked Neil's curiosity. "Did she say why?"

"Trouble sleeping again." Anna sighed. "Don't worry. You guys will settle in soon."

They were all quiet for a moment.

"I'm not worried," Neil lied.

He opened the barn door just as Bree was reaching for it from the other side. She screamed in surprise, causing Neil to cry out a little bit himself. *Watch it!* he wanted to tell her, but before he could say anything, he noticed that his sister looked pale and miserable. The skin below her eyes was dark, and she had a fresh pimple on her nose. "Sorry," he said instead.

Bree pointed toward the computer desk near the far wall. "All yours," she said, brushing by him and stepping toward the house.

"Aunt Anna said you had another nightmare." Bree stopped, keeping her back toward him. "So did I," he continued. "I was being chased through the woods near Graylock. Someone pushed me into the water. . . . I drowned."

Bree turned. What little color was left in her cheeks drained from her face. "I had the same dream," she said quietly, astonished.

Neil had known, somehow, that she was going to say that. "It felt . . ."

"Real," she said. "Like I couldn't breathe. It was terrifying."

"I *couldn't* breathe. I woke up choking. And this morning, I nearly slipped in a puddle of water at the foot of my bed again. Do you think this is the proof we need?" Neil asked, thinking of what Eric had said to him last night: *You're the only one who's seen it.*

"Proof of what?" Bree stared at him blankly.

"Nurse Janet," said Neil. "I'm not the only one who's seen her now. She chased us in the dream. What if she wants to hurt us in real life, just like the legend says?"

"Don't be silly," Bree said with an unconvincing laugh that sounded more like a grunt.

"I'm not being silly. What other answer is there?"

"How's this for an answer . . ." Bree glanced over her shoulder at the house, then lowered her voice even more. "Since Dad hasn't returned my calls for the past couple days, I sent him an e-mail." Neil threw his hands in the air in frustration. "Before you freak out entirely, let me finish. I told him that I didn't want to stay with Aunt Claire and Anna. After what we heard them saying last night, it's obvious that they don't want us here. I asked him if we could go out to California. Live with him instead. Or at least try to figure out some other option. Until Mom . . . you know. Feels better."

For the second time that morning, Neil felt as if he could not breathe — this time out of rage. But he managed to control the tone of his voice. "If living with him was an option, he would have made it happen already, Bree. Don't be stupid. He doesn't want us. And honestly? I don't want him."

"I'm not being *stupid*." Her brow crinkled. Her pimple turned even redder. "I just don't want to be here. Especially with all this stuff going on." She peered over her shoulder into the woods. The trees were cool and unresponsive; save for the breeze in the upper branches, they appeared to taunt by simply ignoring the rest of the anxious world. "I could murder you for making me go to that place."

"To Graylock?" Neil scoffed. "I didn't make you go. As soon as Eric showed up, you practically dragged *me*!"

"My big mistake," Bree said. Neil wasn't sure if she was talking about the trip to the hospital or her brief interest in Eric.

"Fine," said Neil. "But don't come crying to me when Dad writes back and says, 'Sorry, honey, Los Angeles is more expensive than I thought it would be.' Face it. We're stuck here. No running away like Dad. *Or* like Mom. We have to deal with this now. On our own."

"*You* deal with it, then," said Bree. "I'm done. No more nightmares. No more ghosts. I'm going to pick up a nice, fat romance novel from the library and hide out until all this Nurse Janet stuff blows over."

"Blows over? Stuff like this never blows over. *Stuff like this* follows you around. It finds you when you least expect it. The more you ignore it, the worse it gets."

"Yeah, well, you could say that about everything."

"Then you know it's true," said Neil, crossing his arms.

"Whatever, little brother," said Bree, spinning on her heels, walking briskly back toward the house. "Who knows what's true anymore?"

CHAPTER
TWENTY-ONE

LATER, CLAIRE ASKED NEIL AND BREE TO COME to the pie shop with her. Anna had an eleven o'clock phone conference with an art gallery in Woodstock.

Neil decided not to take it personally that Anna clearly wanted them out of her hair. It was just as well. He knew he needed to persuade his sister to help him do something about the strange occurrences — starting with convincing her that he wasn't insane. At least this way they'd be stuck together for the day.

After breakfast, Neil had twenty minutes to get ready. In the upstairs bathroom, he turned on the faucet in the purple claw-foot tub, then twisted the asterisk-shaped knob above the silver spout so that a heavy stream sprayed from the showerhead. Before Neil even had a chance to strip off his shirt and sleep shorts, steam began to rise from the basin where the water was quickly collecting.

The drain must be clogged, Neil thought, stepping into the hot, shallow pool. The previous night's dream flashed briefly through his mind, but then he remembered Bree's attempt to contact their father. His annoyance pushed any other anxiety aside.

If Dad took them away, what would they do about the mystery of Nurse Janet? It would be much more difficult to learn the truth about the asylum in the woods all the way from California. Besides, according to Alexi and Mark, you can't escape a haunting. Spirits travel in the same way memories do. And Neil had been haunted by his parents ever since the beginning of the year — it didn't seem to matter where he went.

Why was Bree insisting on being so blind? How come she refused to place blame where it belonged?

Rick Cady, their father, had lost his job as a high school theater teacher two years ago. He'd looked for work every day until the daily grind grew too exhausting. Then he found solace in rehearsals for *Annie Get Your Gun*, a local production in which he'd been cast as the male lead. It didn't bring in any money, but it made him happy.

Everything changed when, one night, Rick came home late, missing dinner. He explained to his family that he'd met with a casting agent that afternoon in New York City. From the coldness that filled their house over the next few weeks, Neil understood that what was happening between his parents was not merely about acting. Months later, that same agent convinced Rick that Los Angeles was where he needed to be.

Neil believed that everything that had happened since his father went away — this Nurse Janet nonsense included — was his father's fault. The fact that Bree wouldn't admit it was a poison cherry on top of an already toxic sundae. Neil knew what Bree was thinking: *Dad is the only sane parent we have left.* But, Neil wondered, what kind of sane person would leave his family suffering on one side of a continent to go off and pursue a fantasy on the other?

Someone knocked on the bathroom door, snapping Neil back to reality. "We're heading out soon!" It was Claire.

The shower was all steam now. Neil glanced down at his fingertips. They were pruning. "Sorry!" Neil called out, beginning to rinse what was left of the shampoo suds from his hair frantically. "Gimme a minute!" Soapy white residue coated the surface of the water, which had risen halfway up his calves. Neil turned off the faucet, and the water slowed to a trickle from the spout. He swung the shower curtain open and reached for his towel, hanging on a nearby hook.

Wiping his face, Neil felt something brush against his leg. Glancing down at the water, he noticed a ripple of minuscule waves bouncing off the far side of the basin, but the disturbance quieted as quickly as it had begun. The opaque water was difficult to see through, even when Neil bent over to get a closer look.

Something long, thin, and dark squirmed just below the surface.

Neil stood quickly, scrambling to leap from the water. His feet slipped out from under him. His knee hit the edge of the tub, and he toppled to the bathroom floor with a resounding crash. The plush purple bath mat broke his fall, but it didn't stop Claire from rushing back upstairs.

She pounded on the door. "Neil! Are you okay?"

Neil's left shoulder and hip pulsed with a dull pain. He kneeled, his brain scanning the rest of his body. "I tripped," he said, when he was sure he hadn't broken any bones. "Sorry, Aunt Claire."

He cautiously peered over the edge of the tub. The water had dropped a couple inches and had cleared a bit. The bottom of the basin appeared to be empty. Whatever he'd seen moments ago had either been in his imagination, or had slipped down the drain.

"Did you hurt yourself?"

He almost called out to tell Claire what he'd just seen, but the previous night's conversation rose up in his memory. *I'm beginning to wonder if they wouldn't be better off with my brother in Jersey City.* He didn't want to worry her any more than he already had. "I'm fine." He wrapped the towel around him, swiftly wiping away the water that still clung to his skin.

"For goodness' sake, be careful."

By the time Neil was dry, the tub had fully emptied, and he forced himself to peer into the drain itself. The hole lacked a catch-all filter, so he was able to see directly into the pipe below. The water level hovered a few inches down, as if something was, in fact, keeping it from sinking. Closing his eyes and taking a deep breath, Neil reached down. Sticking his finger into the opening, he felt something slimy. Somewhat fuzzy, like a hair clog. Gross, yet familiar.

He managed to catch part of it. He pulled. What came out of the hole made Neil feel faint — a long piece of dark green weed. The kind he'd dreamed about the night before. He dropped it into the tub, where it landed with a disheartening *splat*.

Slipping quickly into his clothes, Neil went out into the hall-way. "Aunt Claire? Aunt Anna?" he called out. Moments later, Claire peeked out from her bedroom door. "Can you come here?" he asked.

Neil turned around and swung the bathroom door wide. "There was another piece of lake grass. This time in the tub. I thought you should —" But, of course, the tub was now empty. Of course. Claire raised an eyebrow, and Neil's skin prickled with embarrassment. The feeling reminded him of waking from the nightmare the night before. "Sorry," he said quickly, hoping he hadn't just made things worse for himself. "I guess I'm seeing things."

CHAPTER
TWENTY-TWO

NEIL AND BREE RODE SILENTLY in the backseat of Claire's car as she drove into Hedston. He did not speak of the bathroom again. When they arrived, the pie shop employees greeted them with enthusiasm. Neil asked Claire if he could use the shop's phone.

An hour later, Wesley arrived on his bike. The boys sat on the curb out front. Neil told him about the lake weed appearing and then disappearing. "I'm getting sort of jealous," said Wesley. "Why hasn't anything strange happened to me or Eric?"

"You want strange?" Neil raised an eyebrow. "You can have some of mine. I don't know how much more I can take."

Wesley kicked a pebble into a nearby storm drain. "You guys can stay at my house if you want. We don't have a lot of room, but I'm sure my mom wouldn't mind."

"This isn't about our *house*." Neil smacked Wesley's knee. "It's about me and Bree. Besides, your mom doesn't even know us."

"I told her about you, though. She thinks it's great that we're hanging out. Other kids in this town . . . well, let's just say they think I'm a little weird."

Neil managed to laugh. "Only a *little*?"

Wesley thought about it, then he laughed too. "Yeah. They haven't seen anything yet."

"Everyone can be weird if you watch them long enough."

A loud engine rumble echoed from around the shop. Seconds later, a large pickup truck roared out of Jameson Way — the thin, alley-like road at the nearest corner — and screeched to a halt in front of them.

Neil pulled his feet out of the front tires' path just in time. He was about to shout a piece of his mind, when a familiar face peered down at him from the driver's window.

"Whoa, there," said Andy. "Almost gotcha! Sorry!"

Immediately, Neil felt bad for what he'd been thinking. Andy opened the door and stepped onto the curb. He held out both hands to the boys and helped them up. "Neil," he said, shaking his head in what appeared to be astonishment. "You're just the person I was looking for. And here I was about to run you over!" He pressed his lips together, sheepish. "Don't tell your aunts. They'll torture me." He nodded hello at Wesley. Wesley nodded back.

"I won't say a word," said Neil, smiling slightly. "You were looking for me?"

"I feel awful about the other night," said Andy. "At the party." Neil felt his lungs tighten. "I know you heard us all talking. . . . I wanted to apologize." Neil didn't say a word. "Whatever is going on with your parents —" Andy stopped himself and glanced uncertainly at Wesley. "Your personal life is none of my business." He reached into the pocket of his jeans, pulled out a scrap of paper, and handed it to Neil. "But, having gone through something similar with my own family, I wanted to let you know that if you ever wanted someone to talk to, you know, someone other than your aunts, you can always call me." Neil opened the note to find that Andy had written his phone number. Andy really *had* been looking for him, and he'd come prepared. Neil felt his face flush. "I can meet you here. Anytime."

"Thanks," Neil heard himself say. He folded up the piece of paper and tucked it into the pocket of his shorts. "That's really . . . nice of you."

"I hope I'm not stepping on toes. I'm just close by, that's all." There was something in this old man's eyes, something sad, that reminded him of his family. It was the kind of thing he'd wished his father had said to him back when he was still around.

Neil glanced down at his sneakers. "My toes are fine." Wesley laughed nervously.

Andy smiled, and then reached out for the café door. Holding it open for them, he said, "Now if I don't get some coffee in my stomach soon, you guys will see me turn into a monster. Not pretty. Trust me."

CHAPTER
TWENTY-THREE

AFTER ANDY TOOK HIS EXTRA-LARGE CUP TO GO, the boys asked Claire if they could borrow her computer. They didn't mention that they planned on looking up as much as they could about the history of Graylock.

"I need to place some orders for the shop," said Claire. "But your sister is heading over to the library. You guys can use the computers there instead. If you're back around one, I'll make you some lunch." She didn't even hint that Neil's bathtub stunt that morning had freaked her out. Maybe he was in the clear?

Bree insisted on walking five steps ahead of them. She hadn't said a word to Neil since their fight about their father. Yes, he wanted her help, but if she was so intent on leaving behind the haunts of Hedston, Neil couldn't force her. Let her read her romance novels. He and Wesley had work to do.

The library was a few blocks ahead. It sat across the street from the expansive hillside view where Neil had first experienced Wesley's Green Man. One story tall, the building had been constructed in the nineteen thirties from local stone of varying size and color. It reminded Neil of a life-sized gingerbread house in a fairy tale. He wondered how the town managed to fit an entire collection of books inside.

As if reading his mind, Wesley said, "There's a big basement. Totally creepy. The computers are down there."

"Great," said Bree, over her shoulder. "That's exactly where I won't be."

As a car came up the street from behind them, the trio moved farther away from the road. The small red hatchback slowed as it passed them, and someone shouted from the open window, "Hey look! Two freaks and a geek!" Then the car sped off, burping out a lick of grayish exhaust.

"Eat dirt!" Wesley stepped forward and shouted. After the sputter of the engine disappeared past the top of the hill, Wesley realized that both Neil and Bree were staring at him in confusion. "Members of my brother's band," Wesley explained. "They've been harassing us the past few days."

"That's terrible," said Bree, looking truly concerned. "Is Eric okay?"

"Eric seems to be handling it fine," said Wesley. "And, uh, I am too, in case you were wondering." He raised an eyebrow, and Bree blushed. "Just gotta stand up for ourselves a little more now. But that's all right. I'm used to it even if Eric isn't."

"What happened between them? Eric and the band, I mean," Neil asked.

"I'm sure it had something to do with a girl," Wesley said, rolling his eyes. "It always does."

Bree cleared her throat and pulled a loose strand of hair behind her ears. "Well," she said in a strange, businesslike tone, "I hope he's able to sort it out."

"Yeah, me too," said Wesley. "I'm all for prank phone calls and everything, but not when I'm the one who's getting them. I mean,

I know what me and Eric are dealing with is nothing compared to the scary stuff that's been happening to you guys, but —"

Bree cut him off with a deathly glance that told him she didn't want to talk about it. "Let's just go."

Once they reached the library steps, Neil said, "The one question I have is: Who of us are the freaks, and which one's the geek?"

"Personally?" said Wesley, taking two steps at a time. "I'd be proud to be called either."

CHAPTER
TWENTY-FOUR

THE LIBRARY WAS COOL AND DARK, the exact opposite of the day they'd left behind outside. A circular wooden desk sat in front of the main entrance; a sign directed patrons to approach at the right for returns, and to check out on the opposite side. A young man sitting at the front looked up from a book he'd been reading. "Hi, Wesley," he said, smiling. He wore a rumpled, collared shirt and a too-short tie, looking as if he'd raided his grandfather's wardrobe.

"Hi, Jay. These are my friends Neil and Bree. They're visiting from New Jersey."

"Welcome to Hedston," said Jay the librarian, in a way that hinted there was no way to feel welcome in this town. "Try to make yourselves comfortable."

"We're heading down to the computers," said Wesley, grabbing Neil's elbow. "Maybe you can tell Bree where to find the romance novels."

Bree's eyes went wide with embarrassment. "Or *anything* really," she said quickly.

"Fiction's over there," said Jay, nodding toward the shelves near the back windows.

Bree whispered to the boys, "Come get me when you guys are done. Aunt Claire gave me her library card, Neil, so if there's a book you need, we can check out together."

❖

On the lower level, two computers sat on a table behind the stair-case. The room was damp and the lights were dim. There were no windows, just the building's stone foundation. Every few seconds, a squeak rose from a corner of the room. Someone was pushing a cart, reshelving books. Otherwise, the boys seemed to have the entire floor to themselves.

Thump!

The cart must have crashed into one of the bookshelves. A soft voice said, "Excuse me." Neil didn't know if the person speaking was talking to them or to the books.

"Let's look her up, then," said Wesley.

"Who?"

"Who else? Nurse Janet!"

But a quick Internet search didn't give them much of a return: several options for Janet Reillys, but none were nurses and none were in Hedston.

"Weird," said Neil. "You'd think someone would have posted something about the legend somewhere."

Wesley modified the search — he tried adding the words *Graylock Hall*, *murders*, *suicide*. Still, the search engine refused to cooperate.

"This is so strange," said Wesley. "According to the Interwebs, the Nurse Janet lady never existed."

"Oh, she existed, all right," said a voice from behind them.

The boys spun their chairs to find a tall, thin woman standing over them. She was dressed in a black jersey dress that was coated with strands of long white cat fuzz. Her gray hair was tied loosely into a lopsided bun on top of her head. Neil thought she looked familiar but didn't know why.

"In fact, she exists still," the woman went on, folding her arms, revealing sharp, red fingernails. "Despite the tall tales folks in this town tell, Nurse Janet Reilly is very much alive."

CHAPTER
TWENTY-FIVE

"We won't tell," said Wesley quickly. "Promise."

The woman stared at the boys in shock.

Neil closed his eyes, mortified.

The woman spoke. "You think that I . . . ?" Then she began to laugh. She laughed so hard, she doubled over, hitching silent gasps before snorting loudly, which sent her into another round of high-pitched giggles. When she found the breath to speak again, she said, "I'm not Janet. Never have been and never will be. I'm Gladys. We met at the party?" Neil nodded. "When I'm not taking classes from your Aunt Anna, I volunteer here at the library. Keeps me cool." Gladys smiled. "Being mistaken for Mrs. Reilly isn't the worst thing people have thought of me. Living in a small town like this, you can make enemies fairly quickly. Folks *love* to talk. I assume that's how the rumors of poor Janet started."

"She's still alive?" Neil said in disbelief.

This changed everything. The nightly visitor. The dream of drowning. The woman in white at the playground. If it wasn't the ghost of Nurse Janet, then who or what was it?

Finding his voice again, Wesley asked, "Can you tell us anything about her?"

"I never met the woman myself. She was a friend of my older sister." Gladys shoved the long, black sleeves of her dress up her bony forearms, looking serious, as if she had been waiting to set the record straight for quite some time. "I know the stories the kids tell in the school hallways. My nieces and nephews used to insist that Janet Reilly was the boogeywoman of Hedston, a vengeful spirit who would haunt trespassers at the asylum in the woods. I think they just liked to scare one another at slumber parties. They refused to listen to the truth."

"Those stories are still around," said Neil, glancing harshly at Wesley, who shrugged apologetically.

"It's all very dramatic." Gladys nodded. "And everyone loves a good spook. No? The truth of the matter is quite simple. There were several drownings out at Graylock. The state investigated. They shut the place down. Many people lost their jobs. Yes, there was some suspicion placed on the staff who worked in the youth ward. But nothing was ever proven. Janet Reilly left this town in a smoke screen of accusation. Folks were so angry that she was able to simply walk away, it's no wonder they demonized her. Poor old thing."

"But what if she was guilty?" asked Wesley.

"That's not really for us to decide, is it?" said Gladys. "She was never charged with a crime."

Wesley said, "But that doesn't mean —"

"Do you know where we can find her?" Neil interrupted. "Talk to her maybe?"

Gladys flinched, surprised. "Now why would you want to go and do a thing like that?" Neil and Wesley looked at each other, silently trying to come up with an answer that would satisfy her. But Gladys only rolled her eyes. "Oh, I know you boys went out to Graylock Hall this week. No need to lie to old Gladys. I was young once too. You're curious about the ghost story. You want to ask Janet yourself?"

Neil's cheeks flushed, but he nodded anyway. "Please don't tell anyone."

Gladys shrugged, teasing, pushing her book cart back into the shadows. The wheels whined in dismay. "There's a retirement home several miles north," she said. "Whispering Knoll, I think it's called. Mrs. Reilly lives there. But you didn't hear it from me."

CHAPTER
TWENTY-SIX

AFTER LOOKING UP THE RETIREMENT HOME'S PHONE NUMBER, the boys closed out of the Internet and made their way back upstairs.

"Did you find what you were looking for?" Jay asked, still sitting behind the circular desk, his book in hand.

"And more," said Wesley. Turning toward Neil, he whispered, "We should get to a phone. Maybe your aunt will let us use the one back at the shop."

Neil nodded, even though he was almost terrified to find out what a living, breathing Nurse Janet would have to say to them. Would she be angry? Would she hang up? He still couldn't believe she was really alive. Was Gladys telling the truth?

Wesley went off to find the bathroom.

"Ugh! Come on!" came a voice from behind a bookshelf near the fiction section.

Jay glanced at Neil. He raised an eyebrow. "She's been doing that for a while."

Neil peeked around the corner and found Bree standing at a computer kiosk. She was looking through the electronic catalogue. "What's the matter?"

Bree stiffened, then turned. She shook her head and waved dramatically at the screen. "This stupid thing isn't working. I keep typing in book titles, and all that pops up are these weird screen savers. Three pictures. When I move the mouse, they go away, but the computer won't let me look for my books."

Neil's throat tightened. "What kind of pictures?"

"I'll show you." Bree searched for a random title, and when she hit enter, a full-screen slide show began. When Neil saw the first photograph, he covered his mouth in shock. It was the same picture he'd seen in his camera's view screen the day before. The taxidermic deer head. When the next photo popped up on the screen, Neil felt dizzy. The piano bench with the stack of sheet music. The third photo — birch logs in a fireplace — was no surprise. Bree stared at him, worried.

Neil felt a hand on his shoulder. He jumped and spun around, lashing out, nearly slapping Jay in the face. The librarian leapt backward. "Whoa!" he said. "I came to see if the catalogue was giving you problems."

"Sorry!" said Neil. "I just thought —"

"As a matter of fact," Bree said, turning back to the screen, "the catalogue *is* giving us problems. A screen saver keeps popping up. The computer won't let me search."

"This machine doesn't have a screen saver," said Jay, confused.

"Well, look," said Bree. She went through the search process again, but this time, after she hit ENTER, the catalogue showed her a list of titles similar to the one she'd entered. No photos. No slide show. "What the heck? It's not doing it now."

Jay sighed and shrugged. "I'm not sure what to tell you, except that the V. C. Andrews books are all right behind you. That's what you were looking for. Right?"

Bree looked sheepish. "Yeah. Thanks."

❖

On the walk back to the pie shop, Neil filled in Wesley about the three photos they'd encountered at the computer kiosk.

"At first, I didn't realize that I was looking at the same pictures Neil saw yesterday," said Bree, "but when I saw Neil's reaction . . ."

"It's like someone was able to tap into the devices," said Neil, "to show us something they wanted us to see. The antlers, the piano bench, and the fireplace."

"But how is that possible?" asked Wesley. "Can you remotely manipulate a camera's memory card? Or a whole library catalogue?"

"Not that I've ever heard," said Bree.

"You know what this means, right?" said Neil. "Bree and I have both dreamed of the lake. We've both seen the weeds. And now, we've both experienced the three photos. Eric's wrong — this is definitely not only in my imagination."

Bree squinted, seeming to concentrate on the sidewalk ahead of her. "Someone wanted us to see these images. *Us*. And somehow they managed to make it happen."

Neil remembered what Alexi and Mark had said about the dead being able to use physical energy in order to show themselves to the living. Maybe the images were simply another way that this spirit, or *whatever*, was trying to communicate with them. But what was it trying to say?

"The antlers, the piano bench, and the fireplace," Bree continued dreamily, seeing the images in her mind. "They've got to mean something. Maybe the pictures have to do with that Nurse Janet legend."

"*Yeah*," said Neil slowly, cautiously, thinking about the news Gladys had revealed to them a few minutes ago. "About that . . ."

PART TWO

❖

DROWNING DREAMS

CHAPTER
TWENTY-SEVEN

BY THE TIME THEY RETURNED FROM THE LIBRARY, Neil and Wesley had filled in Bree on Gladys's story.

They stood uncertainly in front of the shop, waiting for one of them to make the next move. "Something feels wrong," said Bree. She began to shake her head, and Neil knew they had a problem. "I think we should leave it alone."

Neil threw his hands in the air. "A few minutes ago you were all for figuring this out."

"Yeah, but that was before I learned the truth! Nurse Janet is alive — a far cry from being a murderous ghost."

Neil rolled his eyes. *Far cry?* "That only means we have more questions than before."

Wesley nodded. "We have to *do* something."

"And what's that? Call an old woman in a nursing home? Please!" Bree held up the thick book she'd borrowed from the library, *Petals on the Wind*. "I just want to forget all of this, sit by myself and read."

"Where? In California?" Neil spat.

"You guys!" Wesley stepped between them. "Stop." He took a breath. "If Bree doesn't want to be part of it, Neil, then you and me can call Mrs. Reilly. It's fine."

"Thank you, Wesley," said Bree, glaring at her brother. She sat down on the sidewalk beside the shop's front door and practically shoved her nose into the paperback book.

Inside, Neil and Wesley asked Claire if they could use the phone. She was busy with a customer at the register, so she didn't even blink before saying yes. They crept to her office and called the number that Neil had written down at the library. A bored-sounding woman answered. With his heart racing, Neil asked if the woman could connect him to Janet Reilly's room, and she immediately put him on hold. Seconds later, she informed him that Mrs. Reilly was sleeping. She sounded as if she was about to hang up, but Neil quickly asked if Whispering Knoll accepted visitors. "Until six P.M.," the operator said. Then the line went dead.

"How are we going to get up there?" Neil asked Wesley. "My aunts are busy. And anyway, I don't think they'd take us when we told them who she is."

"I know someone with time on his hands," Wesley said. They made another phone call, then waited in the café for their ride to pull up. Fifteen minutes later, Eric arrived at the curb, behind the wheel of his mother's sedan.

"Where's Bree?" Eric asked, as the two boys slipped into the backseat.

Neil was about to tell him when someone yanked the front passenger door open. Bree peeked inside, her eyes wide, her knuckles white as she dug her fingers into her book's cover. "Where are you guys going?" she asked.

"Where do you think?" said Neil. "We couldn't get through on the phone, so —"

"I'm coming," Bree said and then slid into the front seat. She slammed the door shut.

Eric smiled petulantly. "Well, it's nice to see you too."

"Please. Just . . . drive?" said Bree, peering into the rearview mirror.

Eric put the car in gear and pulled away from the curb. "As you wish," he said.

"What made you change your mind?" Wesley asked.

Bree huffed a sigh. She sounded annoyed. "I saw something," she mumbled.

"Something?" Eric said, curious.

"Some*one*." Bree buckled her seat belt. "When I was reading, I felt like I was being watched. I looked up . . ." She shivered, remembering. "A girl was standing across the street, in the alley. I couldn't see her too well, but I noticed she was dressed in a white dress, like a hospital uniform."

"Just like the woman I saw near the playground," said Neil.

"The girl I saw looked like she could have been any age, I guess, but something told me she was around my age. I heard a voice in my head, as if from the other side of a bad phone connection."

"What did it say?" Wesley asked, as if this was a perfectly natural occurrence.

Bree hung her head. "She said, 'Go.'"

"Go?" said Neil. "As in, *with us*?"

Bree nodded. "I stood up and shouted at her to leave me alone. And she was gone. But a second later, my legs went numb. Then my hands. The most incredible pain raced all over my body, like knives cutting my skin. I couldn't breathe. And everything started to go dark." Her voice hitched, but she continued. "I heard her voice again, as if from far away, screaming, 'Go!' So I promised I

would. I said it out loud. And it stopped. She left me alone."
Suddenly furious, Bree turned toward the backseat. "I hate this,
Neil! What have you gotten us into?"

A half hour later, Eric continued north on the twisted country
roads that led to the town of Heaverhill, where Whispering Knoll
Rest Home was located.

"I forgot to tell Aunt Claire we were leaving," said Bree,
clutching her hands in her lap.

"Me too," said Neil, feeling light-headed. This was the first
thing she'd said to him since yelling at him, but it gave him no
comfort.

"If they give you a hard time," said Eric, "I'll tell your aunts I'm
a really good driver."

"Thanks," Bree answered dryly. "I'm sure that'll help." Stone-
faced, she glanced out the window at the immense green fields that
sped by in a dizzying blur. The mountainous horizon from which
they'd come faded in the humid air behind them. Despite the car's
open windows, Neil's forehead was dripping with sweat, and his
teeth nearly chattered with nerves.

"How much longer?" Wesley asked.

As if in response, a small white sign appeared along the side of
the road up ahead. WELCOME TO HEAVERHILL. After another
couple miles, they came to another sign, this one for the rest home.
Neil clutched at his seat belt as Eric made the turn into the long
driveway.

The building was nice, or at least it was nicer than Neil had
expected. He'd heard nursing homes could be depressing, but

Whispering Knoll looked like a giant dollhouse, with gables and spires and white vinyl siding that resembled real wood.

After parking, the four approached the main entrance. A pair of dark glass doors slid open. The group went in together, silent and curious. A quiet desk, covered in colorful flowers, stood off to the right of a wide foyer. A short woman greeted them with a fake-looking smile. "Can I help you?" she asked.

"We're here to see Janet Reilly," said Neil. "I called earlier but she was sleeping."

"And you are?" the woman asked, waiting for him to finish the sentence.

"Friends," said Bree. Neil was glad that she had his back. "Came up for a visit."

The woman behind the desk sighed heavily, as if they'd asked her to run a marathon. She typed something into her computer. "Looks like she's scheduled for the rec room right now. But she's already got a visitor in there. Her son comes every afternoon." She glanced up at the group.

Neil smiled, pretending to be unperturbed. "It'll be nice to see him too. Which way do we go?"

The receptionist seemed surprised and a bit disappointed at his quick response, but pointed down the hall. "Straight ahead. Can't miss it."

Wesley leaned toward the desk. "And, uh, could you tell us what she looks like?"

Bree smacked Wesley on the back. He cried out, and Bree forced a laugh. The receptionist wore a look that said she might call Security. "Such a kidder," Bree said. The group hurried off toward a pair of French doors.

"Smooth move, guys," Eric said.

"I was just trying to help," said Wesley.

The rec room was large, bright, and comfy. Soft couches were set up facing each other in several areas. On an enormous television in a far corner, a muted game show played. A pool table stood in the center of the room, flanked by two unoccupied Ping-Pong tables. Most of the residents who were there seemed happy to simply sit near the sunny windows, enjoying the view of a sloping green hillside.

A middle-aged man, younger than most of the people in the room, walked briskly toward them. Neil worried that the man was about to kick them out, but he passed them by.

Neil, Bree, Wesley, and Eric were now alone with a group of elderly people. Slowly, the four stepped forward.

Two women sat off to the left of the space, engaging in what sounded like a deep conversation about the weather. One man held onto a walker, staring silently out the window. A fourth woman was perched in a wheelchair. Her back was toward them. An empty chair sat beside her.

Neil thought of the man who'd passed them at the center of the room . . . the receptionist's news that Mrs. Reilly had a visitor . . . the chair that seemed to wait for someone's return. He approached this woman, her broad shoulders greeting him like a wall; her thin gray hair cut short, styled in mashed curls. "Mrs. Reilly?" he said.

She turned and saw the group standing behind her. Her face was weathered, her laugh lines deep. Her bottom lip quavered, and for a moment, Neil wondered if she was crying. But she wasn't.

The movement seemed to be a spasm. It ended when the woman showed a smile that lit up her blue eyes. "Yes?" she said.

"My name is Neil Cady," he said, keeping his voice even, though his insides trembled. Imagining how someone on a detective show might sound, he said, "This is my sister, Bree, and my friends Wesley and Eric. We were wondering if we could talk to you for a few minutes?"

"About what?" she asked, her brow crinkling.

"About Graylock Hall," said Neil. The words fell from his mouth like a stone into water. They seemed to ripple through the room, slowly making their way to the old woman's ears.

When Janet Reilly finally processed what he'd said, her smile dropped away, and those bright blue eyes seemed to cloud over, as if a storm were brewing somewhere deep inside.

CHAPTER
TWENTY-EIGHT

"WHAT ABOUT IT?" MRS. REILLY ASKED, but her puckered face told them she knew exactly what they wanted to hear. She sighed and rolled her eyes. "Sit down," she said, as if she'd been dreading this moment for many years. "Quick. Before my son gets back."

The four grabbed several stools from a nearby card table and arranged them around the old woman's wheelchair. When they were settled, Neil felt as if they were attending some sort of messed-up story time at his hometown library back in New Jersey.

"You wanted to see Nurse Janet for yourselves?" Mrs. Reilly's face grew darker, angrier. "Isn't that how the story goes? Old Janet Reilly. The Monster of Graylock Hall?" She leaned toward Wesley, as close as she could get. Her breath was orange scented — even Neil could smell her from where he sat. *"Aren't you scared of me?"* she whispered, a lightning flash in her eye. Anger? Amusement? She was difficult to read.

"Should we be?" asked Eric, crossing his arms, refusing to play her game.

Mrs. Reilly sat back and took him in. After a few seconds, she exhaled, releasing her intensity like steam from a kettle of boiling water. "Of course not," she said honestly. "I never hurt anyone in my life. So why do you kids insist on turning me into a monster?"

"That's not what we came to do," said Bree.

"If you tell us about Graylock," Neil tried, "we can share the truth with our friends."

"The truth?" Mrs. Reilly laughed a humorless laugh. "You came here, so you must know the story . . . though I doubt your version has much to do with the truth." She shrugged. "Short version: Some patients died while under my watch. The town blamed me." She paused again. "They said that I was responsible."

"But you're not?" Bree whispered.

"That's the big question, isn't it?" Mrs. Reilly answered, more softly than any of them expected. "You want the truth?" She coughed, cleared her throat, and then shook her head, which appeared heavy, weary with memory. "The truth is: The patients did it to themselves, honey. Remember, these kids were not well. They had emotional problems. Addictions. Difficult families. These were good kids who needed help. They deserved the best kind of treatment, but what they got was Graylock. And they wanted *out*.

"We all knew that when the summer storms came through that place," she continued, looking each of them in the eye in turn, "the island's power grid usually failed, and the back door of the youth ward would unlatch. I begged my bosses to get it fixed, but considering the condition of the rest of the building, one little broken door didn't seem to be high on their list of priorities, even after the second time it happened. The investigations. The accusations. The poor patients . . ." The old woman sighed.

"That's so horrible," said Bree, shivering beneath the air-conditioning vent.

"I worked the graveyard shift alone," Mrs. Reilly went on, "unlucky enough to be in the position where my kids were capable of sneaking out from under my watch. And let me tell you, when the lights went out in that building, it was all I could do to keep track of *myself*, never mind fifteen teenagers no older than the lot of you."

"So the drownings really *were* accidents?" said Neil. He thought of the nightmare he'd had — running through the woods, falling into the lake, trapped under the surface, inhaling water. He knew it had been a dream, because he'd been asleep, but upon waking it had seemed so very much like a memory, as if it had really happened. As if he'd been one of the patients.

There was one big difference between Mrs. Reilly's explanation and what he'd seen: In the dream, someone had been chasing him.

Mrs. Reilly clutched at the arms of her chair, her eyes suddenly wild. "Don't think I haven't blamed myself every day for what happened. It hurts. To fail those in your care despite your best intentions. To have an entire community turn against you . . . To have friends and family wondering: Is it true? Is she capable of such an atrocity?" She calmed herself, glancing at her audience as if they'd suddenly materialized all around her. "I'm sorry. . . . You didn't come to hear this."

"We did, actually," said Eric.

"And *we're* sorry," Bree added. "It must have been horrible for you."

Mrs. Reilly nodded. "Deep down, they may have known I was no villain." Her words now seemed to bubble forth, uncontainable. "I believe with my heart and soul that the people of Hedston never wanted to blame me alone, but who else did they have to blame? No one else was there."

Again, Neil had a feeling she was wrong: *Someone* was there — the person who'd chased him in his dream.

Still, Mrs. Reilly sniffed, disgusted at her recollection. "No one did a thing to help. No one spoke up in my defense. How much easier had it been for them to run me out of town than to attack a mundane evil — the kind that is born of neglect and denial?"

"So you moved away," said Wesley carefully. "Did you ever go back to Hedston?"

"No," said Mrs. Reilly. "Why should I, when the memory of that town has followed me all these years? Even now, I am there. . . ." She blinked, as if forcing herself back into her body. "I believe we must all share the guilt for the tragedies that occurred at Graylock Hall. If I'm a demon, then so is everyone who sat back and did nothing, while that building fell apart with those poor people in it." She reached out and grabbed Neil's wrist. Her fingers were cold; he stiffened, but forced himself not to pull away. "You said you'd tell your friends the truth." Neil nodded, staring at her trembling lip. "Promise," she whispered.

"Mom?" The man had returned. He stood just outside of the small powwow circle. "Are you okay?"

Mrs. Reilly glanced at her son as if coming out of a dream. "Oh. Nicholas. Are you done with your call?"

"All set," said the man, his hands in the pockets of his black jeans. He looked at the group, realization dawning in his eyes. His brow darkened. His bloodshot eyes filled with loathing.

Neil felt the room start to spin. It would all be over in a moment. He patted the old woman's hand. "I promise," he said. "I do, but I have one more question." He knew he had to spit out this next part or else it would lodge in his throat. "Do you believe in ghosts?"

Nicholas Reilly stepped forward. Raising his voice, he said, "What's this about?"

"Ghosts?" Mrs. Reilly asked, confused. She dropped Neil's hand. "What kind of ghosts?"

Neil glanced at her son, whose chest seemed to be growing larger. "We've been seeing . . . a girl."

"You're kidding," said Nicholas. "Not a *girl*! How terrifying for you."

Bree spoke up, ignoring him. "Do any of these things mean anything to you?" She mentioned the deer antlers, the piano bench, the white logs in the fireplace.

Mrs. Reilly only stammered, "N-not that I can recall. Why?"

Nicholas grabbed the handles on the back of his mother's wheelchair. "Let's get you back up to your room. You've had enough excitement for one day."

"Well, I'd like to have some more, if you don't mind," Mrs. Reilly said, glancing up at her son. As he pushed her chair away, she reached out and grabbed his arm. "I want to ask them something." Nicholas sighed, but turned the chair around so that Mrs. Reilly faced the group once more. "Where are you from?" she asked.

Neil stood up. He suddenly felt terrible about barging in to the nursing home. He owed her an explanation. "Bree and I are visiting our aunts in Hedston for the summer. Wesley and Eric live there too. We'd heard the stories. We were curious to meet you. Sorry. We didn't mean to cause any trouble."

Mrs. Reilly nodded, seeming to forget how upset she'd been moments earlier. "I do like guests. I don't get nearly enough of them." Nicholas rolled his eyes. "Your visit was a surprise, but I'm happy to set the record straight." She smiled at each of them. Then she tilted her head and glanced around the space. "Where's the other one?" she asked.

Neil, Bree, Wesley, and Eric looked at one another in confusion.

"What other one?" Neil asked.

Mrs. Reilly sat up straight, grabbing the wheels of her chair and turning herself around, taking in all of the room. Nicholas stepped back. "The other girl you came in with. She was just here." She let go of the wheels and drifted a few inches forward. "My sight isn't too good, but I'm sure she had long dark hair. Dressed in white. Never said a word."

Neil grabbed at his sister's hand. Bree squeezed back. He felt the same way he had back in room 13, when the ghostly shape had begun to appear in the darkness. His stomach lurched. He wanted to run, but to where? From what?

The old woman looked toward the group, concern filling her watery blue eyes. "She was so familiar to me. Where did she go?"

CHAPTER
TWENTY-NINE

THEY RODE HOME IN SILENCE. If Mrs. Reilly believed that there had been another girl with them, then the seat between Bree and Neil would have to be where she now sat. They both made an effort to keep their distance from it. Neil crossed his legs tightly, and Bree hung on to the handle above the car door.

When they passed back into Hedston, Wesley spoke up. "At least she was nice."

"Nice?" said Eric. "Who cares if she was nice. Nice doesn't mean she's not guilty."

"You really think that little old lady was capable of killing those kids?" Bree asked.

"She wasn't always a little old lady," said Eric. "Did you see the size of her shoulders?"

"It doesn't really matter, does it?" said Neil, pressing himself against the door, far away from that center seat. "Someone or something is haunting me and Bree. We might have had a chance to stop the haunts when we assumed the ghost was Nurse Reilly. We had a little information. But now we're back at square one. If something followed us home from Graylock, how do we figure out what it is?"

"We look to the clues," Wesley suggested.

"Which are?" asked Eric.

"The three pictures that keep popping up, for one," said Bree. "The antlers, piano bench, and firewood."

"That doesn't seem like a lot to go on," said Eric, turning onto Tulley Avenue toward the pie shop. "And there's no guarantee that those pictures you guys keep seeing have anything to do with Graylock. It might all be a coincidence."

The group snuck into the shop through the back door. But Neil was barely past the threshold when he heard Claire's voice. "You were gone for quite some time," she called out. Nearly jumping out of his skin, Neil turned with the others to see his aunt at the office desk. She went on, "I thought we were going to ask before taking off from now on." Neil didn't know what to say. He knew they'd broken her rule, but he'd been hoping to find her so occupied that she wouldn't notice. Her head wobbled slightly like their mom's did when she was about to explode. "Well? What do you have to say for yourselves?"

"Blame me, Claire," said Eric. "I had my mother's car. I wanted them to come for a ride. We were too far away before they realized they forgot to ask."

"You could have called."

Neil stepped forward. "We're sorry."

"Are you? Truly? Because you only look scared." She was right — Neil was terrified. He wanted desperately to tell her what had been happening, but he was more frightened about what might happen if she and Anna sent him away. Claire sighed. "I don't blame you. *Everything* must seem scary right now. Change is hard."

She shook her head. "I've been too busy to keep you two busy enough. I want you to have fun up here. And I don't want you to feel like prisoners. So . . . just don't tell your Aunt Anna that I lost track of you. That's better than the alternative. Don't you think?"

Neil felt as if she'd shot him in the stomach. He knew what the alternative was: shipping him off to another relative. Perhaps seeing the pain in Neil's face, Claire quickly changed the subject. "I only noticed you'd left because your father called here looking to speak with you guys."

"He called?" Bree said, perking up. "Did he say anything?"

"Only that he knows he's a *real jerk* for not phoning sooner." She smiled, seeming to take pleasure in calling him that. Neil grinned too. "And that he'd try again tomorrow." Her smile dropped away as she added, "Bree, did you tell him that you didn't want to stay with us anymore?"

Bree's cheeks flushed red. "I only meant . . . that maybe somewhere closer to home might be easier for all of us."

"Oh," said Claire, clearly hurt. "Well, if that's what you guys want —"

"It's not what *I* want," said Neil.

"We'll talk about it later," Claire said, turning back to her computer. Neil couldn't tell if she was still upset. "Shop's closing soon. Anna's cooking. Hungry?"

CHAPTER
THIRTY

At dinner, Anna asked everyone about their day. Bree and Neil looked at each other, while Claire conspicuously shoved a forkful of spinach into her mouth. "It was interesting," said Bree. "We learned a lot."

"About?" Anna asked, her eyebrows dancing. Somehow, she always managed to look at them with suspicion.

"Pie," Claire mumbled. "Right, guys?"

Neil smiled. It wasn't a total fabrication.

After they'd all cleared the dining table and scrubbed the dishes in the sink, the aunts decided to light the citronella torches in the backyard, and they invited Neil and Bree to sit outside, eat ice cream, and watch the sky.

"There's supposed to be a meteor shower this weekend," said Anna, following Claire out the door. "Last year's was spectacular. The falling stars inspired a whole batch of my pottery."

"If it's okay with you all," said Bree, "I'm going to relax upstairs."

Standing out in the dimly lit yard, the aunts glanced at each other, obviously concerned. *And they don't know the half of it,* thought Neil. It had been a strange day. He certainly didn't trust his own brain to behave — should he trust his sister's? But by the time he turned back, Bree had disappeared into the house, and he felt he had no choice but to follow Claire and Anna.

As the three sat in the metal lawn furniture out back, the chirping of the crickets and tree frogs became so loud that the aunts' conversation was nearly drowned out. Neil didn't care; he wasn't listening anyway. The world vibrated all around him, and for the first time in a long time, he felt somewhat okay in it. No need to escape in stories. No need to hide away in legends.

Back at the house, the sound of running water came from an upstairs window. Bree was taking an evening bath — a habit she'd had since he could remember. He forced the memory of his own traumatic bathtub experience out of his mind.

He licked voraciously at the cone that Aunt Anna had prepared for him, trying to catch the mint-chocolate-chip ice cream before it leaked down onto his fingers.

For the first time all summer, Neil allowed himself to think of his mother. He wondered where she was right now. A month ago, he would have been sitting on her bed with her, her face smashed into a damp pillow, her blond hair sprawled like a cobweb halo. He would have stroked her back as she held in the sobs he knew she'd hidden from him when he'd entered the room. Whenever he found her like that, he didn't know what to do. She'd asked him not to tell anyone how she was feeling, but it had gotten harder and harder, especially when she seemed too tired to even lift her head to glance at him.

Alexi and Mark said that ghosts don't like things to change. A haunting might simply be a soul's inability to make peace with the past. Ghosts can't see forward; they only look back. Just like his mom.

It seemed silly to call the police because your mother was too sad. He would have done just that if Bree hadn't called their father instead and told him what was going on. Neil was almost excited at the prospect of his father having to come home and finally deal with this situation. But when Neil learned his father's solution — that he and Bree would stay with the aunts — he'd felt as if his head might explode with anger.

Looking up from his cone, Neil was surprised to see his aunts dancing like hippies in the torchlight. There was no music except for their laughter. They twirled and raised their arms to the speckled sky, as if calling for the stars to fall. When they noticed Neil watching, they ran to him and pulled him up, causing his cone to drop into the grass. He began to protest, but when Anna spun him, he relented, becoming entranced by her giddiness. She clasped his shoulders, bringing him to a halt; then, with one finger, she raised his chin. "Look," she whispered.

Dozens of white streaks, each lasting less than a second, dashed across the dark dome above them. Neil felt something strange moving inside his head, a buzzing type of burn. Then, before he knew it, his eyes filled with tears, and all the stars crashed in one big blur.

A scream filled the night. It took Neil a moment to realize where it came from. The aunts turned toward the house too. The light in the upstairs bathroom looked stark, alone. "Help me!" Bree cried out, before screaming again.

When the sound of her voice cut off abruptly, Neil was jolted out of his trance. He forgot the stars, forgot his mother, forgot everything, and ran toward the dark house.

CHAPTER
THIRTY-ONE

HE QUICKLY REACHED THE BACK STEPS. The door. The kitchen. The foyer. The stairs. The hallway. The bathroom.

Neil tried the knob but it wouldn't budge. He pounded the door as hard as he could, rattling the surprisingly strong wood. "Bree?" He pictured his sister on the other side, sprawled on the floor, a pool of blood spreading out on the tile below her cracked skull, the window smashed, a blur of white, someone slipping outside into the night. "Bree!" he shouted again, so loud that his throat hurt.

Neil felt a presence behind him and turned to find the aunts hurrying to catch up. Claire and Anna picked up the shouting where he'd left off. "Bree? Honey? Open the door!" Seconds ticked by. Neil began to feel numb, pins and needles creeping up his arms from the tips of his fingers, like poison spreading toward his heart. He heard Claire say something — *Should we break it down?* — but he didn't know who she was speaking to.

"Bree!" he tried again, calling his sister's name so hard he thought he might break.

Then, from the other side of the door, a voice came. Softly. "Yes?" Bree answered.

Neil and his aunts were so stunned, none of them spoke for several seconds. Eventually, Claire managed to ask, "Is everything okay in there?" Neil clenched his jaw. How many times had he heard that question over the past few days?

There was a rustling at the knob, then the door opened a crack. Neil pushed it ajar, accidentally knocking it into his sister. "Hey!" she said. "Watch it!" She stood beside the draining bathtub, a plush pink towel wrapped around her torso, her brown hair stuck to her forehead. "Ever hear of privacy?"

"What were you screaming about?" Neil asked. His heart was still knocking in his chest and would probably keep going on that way for the rest of the night.

Bree glanced at the bathtub. Expressionlessly, she said, "I fell asleep. I had a dream." Met by horrified stares, she seemed to suddenly understand the havoc she'd created. "Sorry!"

Anna stepped forward, peering into the bathroom, as if she too wondered whether Bree was really alone in there. "You can't do that, honey," she said. "Fall asleep in the bathtub? Don't you realize you could have drowned?"

Bree maintained those cool eyes, that thin smile. "No, I guess I didn't realize." She sighed. Neil heard a slight trembling in her chest as her breath escaped her lungs. "Look, I'm really sorry. I won't do it again. Showers only for me from now on. Okay?"

Claire shook her head, then reached out and stroked Bree's wet head. Bree stepped back, and when Claire pulled her hand away, a long green strand stretched off from Bree's hair. Wide-eyed, Bree snatched the lake weed from her aunt's grip, crumpling it up and hiding it behind her.

"What the heck was that?" asked Anna.

Bree blinked, looking numb. "A special scalp treatment. Keeps my hair really glossy."

LATER THAT NIGHT, after everyone had found their way to their bedrooms, Neil lay looking at the ceiling above his bed until he was certain the rest of the house had finally gone dark. Then he pulled back his sheets and crept to the door. The hallway was a mess of shadows, but he managed to find his way to Bree's room. He didn't knock. Pushing open the door, Neil gasped.

Bree was sitting on top of her bedspread in the darkness. Light shined through the window, up from the porch lamp below, marking a dim yellow swatch on the ceiling and softly illuminating her face. Bree watched Neil watching her, as if she had expected him to come.

He closed the door and made his way to the end of her bed. "Are you okay?" he asked. "Really?" Bree shook her head, and Neil climbed up next to her. "What happened? What did you see?"

Bree turned to the window. Neil waited. After what felt like a long time, she said, "I never realized before I came to Hedston how very sad ghost stories are."

"Sad?"

Bree nodded. "Those *Ghostly Investigators* you love so much? They're always getting rid of the spirits. Banishing them, or whatever they call it. Like during the episode we watched the other night, those two guys came swaggering into that place and started telling the people who lived around there that all they had to do was demand the ghosts leave. And the people were happy that they could get on with their lives." Bree looked up from the blanket, right into Neil's eyes. "But what about the ghosts?"

"I don't understand."

"Don't you feel sorry for the ghosts?"

"Not particularly," said Neil. This was just like her — to have sympathy for the bad guy. She was the same way about their father. "Not when they're doing awful things."

Bree shook her head. "Those *Investigator* people talk about ghosts like they're monsters or something," she said, wiping at her eyes. "Creatures that need to be defeated, when, really, they're humans. With memories. And wishes. And fears. And I know that the spirit who followed us home from Graylock has been doing bad things. But she's been doing them for a reason."

Neil felt chills crash like an ocean wave on his back, but he still didn't know what to say.

Bree leaned forward, pulled her damp hair behind her ears. "Tonight, in the bathtub, I didn't fall asleep like I told the aunts."

"Yeah, I figured that."

"I was lying in the water, rinsing my hair, when all of a sudden, I couldn't sit up. Something was holding me down. It felt like a rope was wrapped around my neck."

"Like in the dream we both had the other night?" said Neil, his breath coming out quickly. Bree nodded. "It wasn't rope. It was the lake weed."

"I opened my eyes," she said. "They stung, but I could see that I wasn't in the bathtub anymore. All around me was a kind of darkness that I can't even describe. It was bigger than just the lake. It felt huge, like outer space. I could see a light shining on me from

above. Someone was standing on the shore. Watching. I scrambled
to reach out to the person, but I couldn't move. The weeds held
me. I started to scream.

"Finally, the person crept closer, but instead of helping me,
their hands pressed me deeper into the water. I choked. I thought
I might die. The pins and needles came. It was the most horrifying
pain. I remembered something I heard in biology class: It hurts
like that when you're drowning." Bree hugged herself, shuddering
the thought away. "Then I was back in the bathroom. Sitting up.
Gasping. Moments later I heard you pounding on the door. I tried
to compose myself. I didn't want to scare the aunts."

"You weren't very convincing," Neil said, trying to smile.

"These . . . visions are getting worse," said Bree. "We already
learned that the ghost who followed us home from Graylock Hall
wasn't Nurse Janet. The ghost is one of the patients who drowned
in the lake. What happened *wasn't* an accident. The girl was murdered." Bree took Neil's hand and squeezed. "All these bad things
she's doing, she's not doing to hurt us. She's showing us what happened. She wants us to figure out who killed her."

CHAPTER
THIRTY-THREE

In the morning, Neil called Wesley in a panic. "Come over," he begged. "I need your help."

By the time Wesley pulled into the driveway on his bike, Claire and Anna had disappeared into the barn to clean and organize. It was Sunday. Both of the aunts had taken the day off, so Neil and Bree didn't have to follow either of them into town.

Bree'd been quiet since breakfast, so Neil decided to let her be. Upstairs, she'd picked up her viola for the first time since coming to Hedston. He knew she must be contemplating their late-night conversation. Music helped her think. She practiced her scales, sliding her fingers up and down the chord progressions faster and faster, the music sounding like a swarm of panicked bees.

The boys sat on the front porch, and Neil filled Wesley in.

"Wow," said Wesley afterward. "So your sister thinks this . . . spirit . . . is pointing you toward a killer?" He glanced around, bracing himself against a chill that wasn't there. "What if the killer is still alive?" Wesley spoke slowly, his voice filled with worry. "Say you find out who did it."

"We go to the police."

"And tell them what?"

Neil shook his head, unsure.

"You know I'm into this stuff as much as you are," said Wesley, clenching his hands nervously, "but it sounds dangerous."

Neil stared at the ground at the bottom of the steps. A warm wind rustled the front lawn. He remembered what Bree had said the night before, about all ghost stories being sad, about putting himself in their shoes. For some reason, her comment made him think of his mother, her crying fits, the way she'd insisted she felt alone even as he sat right beside her. He understood now what was happening here. A desperate soul, lost in a downward spiral, had found him, asking for his help. Neil hadn't been able to give it to his mother — in fact, he'd practically run away from her. Now was his chance to do something right.

"I'm sorry," said Wesley. "I don't want anyone to get hurt again. That's all."

Neil glanced at the wilted gauze taped to his shin. "You didn't seem to care about that a couple days ago when you told me about Graylock." He didn't mean to sound unkind, but Wesley still crossed his arms.

"That was different," said Wesley. "It was supposed to be fun. Things have changed." He was quiet for a few moments. Thoughts of the dead girl seemed to fill the air between the boys. Maybe she was here now, listening. "We could try communicating with her. Maybe she'll go ahead and tell us what she needs us to know. I have a Ouija board at home. Or we could do automatic writing."

"I don't know about that. If she could tell us *everything*, don't you think she already would have?" asked Neil, shaking his head. "I feel like this girl must be new at this. She's learning. She can't talk, so she haunts. She's frightened, so she shows us what scares her. She comes when we're most capable of seeing her — at night, in dreams, when our minds are open. She actually *brought* me and Bree to the moment of her death."

"Great," said Wesley, "so if this girl drowns you, I'll remember to tell everyone she didn't mean it."

Neil shook his head, not in the mood for jokes. "All this is only a piece of the puzzle. And you're right, the bigger picture is scarier. Someone killed her at Graylock Hall." *Someone who may still be out there.* The cherry-colored music of Bree's viola drifted out from the window above him, mixing with the breeze, floating off into the woods. Neil hugged his legs close. His own touch stung slightly — a reminder of his last trip into the woods. "That has to be where the answers lie."

CHAPTER
THIRTY-FOUR

NEIL WALKED TO THE TREES at the back of the aunts' property. Wesley reluctantly followed. It would be easier for them to sneak away while Bree played the viola. If anyone asked, they would say they were simply looking for one of those ancient New England rock walls the old farmers had left behind centuries ago, before the lands had changed hands and the fields had become forest.

As the foliage enveloped the view of the large Victorian house behind them, Neil began to feel queasy. Was he really about to do this again? What if the dead girl showed him exactly what he needed to know? And what if he didn't want to know it anymore? Out here, surrounded by a camouflage of green, where animals hid and watched — and possibly stalked — all his talk about *doing something* was leaking out of him like air from a punctured bicycle tire.

"You coming?" said Wesley, crunching through the brush ahead.

"Right behind you," said Neil, ignoring the tremors in his gut.

And then there was Graylock.

The boys helped each other underneath the fence, strolled across the bridge and down the long walk onto the island. When they came around the corner of the building toward the place where they had last entered — that broken basement window — they were surprised to find boards covering the opening. Fresh, glimmering nails penetrated through the new planks into the old window's frame.

"Someone knew we were here," said Wesley.

"Yeah," said Neil. "Looks like they didn't want us to come back."

"I'm not sure which is worse," said Wesley. "A killer ghost? Or a killer-*killer*. Maybe we should take the hint."

Neil peered back past the rows of pines toward the bridge. No one appeared to have followed them, but that didn't necessarily mean the boys were alone. Wesley was right. Maybe this *was* too dangerous.

An odd sensation began to tingle at Neil's toes. It was a numbing feeling, the beginnings of "dead limb," like when you kneel down and cut off the blood supply to your feet.

The girl was nearby, and she wanted them to keep going. What else would she do to spark them onward? Choke them? Blind them? Tangle them in lake weed? Before he could think too much, Neil tugged Wesley's sleeve, pulling him farther along. "The youth ward is this way. Right?" Wesley dragged his heels.

After a long walk, just before the tip of the land met the dark water of the lake, the boys found a broken patio. A half-moon of concrete radiated out from the building. Flowering weeds had grown tall through the cracks in the pavement, obscuring some old hopscotch paint below — a rudimentary sort of playground.

Looking up at the building, Neil recognized the tall windows that stared back at him. The youth ward was on the other side. In the wall to their right was a door. Neil stepped upon the clingy green stalks and made his way to the entry, remembering what Mrs. Reilly had said about this door being broken all the time. He reached out and clasped the handle. When he pulled, the rusted hinges screamed. The darkness inside had been waiting for him.

He turned around to find Wesley staring at him, exuding unease. The boys said nothing as they stepped over the threshold.

They walked quickly up the steps that led up to the main room. Neil pushed open the wire-mesh door. The cake still sat on the table to his right. The air was musty. Nothing had moved. Nothing had changed.

"Now what?" asked Wesley. He glanced at the ceiling, wearing a look of concern. He obviously did not want to go upstairs.

Neil shared his fear. "We saw the girl in room 13. Maybe she'll appear there again."

Wesley shook his head. "She only appeared because she was able to draw from your batteries. Your flashlight and camera."

Neil sighed. They'd left the aunts' house in such a hurry, they hadn't considered that the spirit might need another energy source in order to communicate with them. "Maybe we should poke around down here instead, then. Save me another bloody nose. Where did Eric find that file folder he took last time?"

Wesley nodded at the closed door in the opposite wall, the one beside the cake table. "He came from there. Remember?"

A small window provided enough light to show them that the room was a small office — a nursing station perhaps. A desk was shoved in a corner, piled with junk — folders, a typewriter, a bulky stapler. Tall wooden filing cabinets lined every wall. "The patients' information is all here," Neil said, "or at least, information on the ones who lived in this section of the hospital. Maybe we can find the files of the girls who died?"

"We don't even know their names," said Wesley. "When I looked online, I couldn't come up with anything specific about the deaths. Something about 'confidentiality.'"

Neil caught sight of a metallic object glinting on the desk, buried slightly by dusty office supplies. The object was sharp. A knife maybe? He crept closer. When he touched the tip of it, a wave of relief rushed over him, followed quickly by another one of disappointment. It was only a letter opener.

"Check this out," Wesley said. He pointed to the large pad of paper on which the opener was lying. "A calendar. Maybe someone wrote something down, something we can use."

"Worth a peek, I guess."

The boys cleared away as much stuff as possible so that they had a complete view of the calendar. The yellowed page showed June from twenty years ago. There were several pencil markings, but most were so faint, they were barely legible. Neil leaned close and squinted, trying to read them. "Karen B.'s birthday," he said, pointing to the box marked with the number 5. "That must be the party that happened out in the common room."

Wesley sighed. "Does that mean we should be looking in the files for a Karen B.?"

"It couldn't hurt."

Wesley shrugged. "I don't know about you, Neil, but this is starting to feel like an impossible —" He stopped, turning his head toward the door.

Neil stepped closer to him. "What's wrong?"

Wesley waved him quiet. "I heard something."

Then Neil heard it too. The hinges that had screamed at them from the door downstairs were whining now. The boys weren't alone here after all.

Neil stepped toward the doorway, but Wesley held the back of his shirt, shaking his head. Neil had no intention of walking into the main room; he simply wanted to shut the office door. To hide.

The small window on the opposite side of the room presented the option of a fall to the grass below. Was it worth the risk of breaking his neck?

Peering around the edge of the door, Neil heard footsteps. Wesley clutched Neil's hand as they both watched the top of a head rise past the lip of the stairs inside the cage. Long dark hair, messy, covering her face — a girl in a dirty white dress. Neil remembered a horror novel he'd read several years ago in which a couple of kids were haunted by a gang of evil girls who looked similar to the one rising up before him.

But this wasn't a character from a book.

Wesley pulled Neil back, just as the girl reached for the cage door. They backed up against the desk, knocking into a pile of folders. To their horror, the pile wobbled. It fell, as if in slow motion, and they scrambled to catch whatever they could, but it was too late. The folders fell to the floor, sliding across the room in a straight line, one on top of another, like dominoes, toward the office entrance. The boys held their breath as the sound of the cage door slammed in the main room.

Then a soft voice whispered, "Neil? Wesley? Is that you?"

CHAPTER
THIRTY-FIVE

For a moment, Neil was thrilled and terrified. The ghost knew their names! She'd spoken to them!

Then, as his brain began to work again, he came back down to earth.

"Bree?" he called out grudgingly.

Footsteps sped toward him, echoing in the other room like gunshots. Then his sister's face was in the doorway. She was panting, out of breath. She did not look happy. "What are you two *doing* in here?"

"I could ask you the same question," Neil shot back.

"You left me at home!" Bree stepped into the room, standing on the pile of folders that had sprawled on the floor.

"Sorry," said Neil. "I didn't want to make a scene."

"I saw you head into the woods behind the barn. I didn't think you'd actually come in here again. Are you *insane*?"

"If he's insane," said Wesley, "we're all insane."

Neil looked around, the evidence of the building's history piled up everywhere. "We need to help her." The word *her* hung between them, like the humming of a struck bell.

After a moment, Bree shook her head. "No. We don't. What we need to do is ignore all this and go. Come on."

"After everything we talked about last night? After everything you said?"

Bree closed her eyes. A glimmer of guilt wrinkled her fore-head. "Yeah, well, I gave it some more thought, and I realized that my sanity and my safety are more important than helping some dead girl I've never met."

Neil clenched his jaw. "You're lying." Bree glared at him. "I know you. I've seen how much this is bothering you." She crossed her arms. Her face told him that he was right.

A metallic squeal sounded from the common room, followed by a loud bang. The three froze, standing wide-eyed in the office.

"You came alone, right?" Wesley whispered to Bree. She nod-ded sharply.

That queasy feeling gurgled in Neil's stomach again. He thought of sharp metal objects, glinting in gloved hands, carried by a killer. Trying to calm himself down, he said, "There might be a simple explanation." Then he stepped forward, twisting away from his sister's grasp, and forced himself to peek out the door.

One of the chairs had toppled over, as if someone had kicked it away from the cake table, but that was not what captured Neil's attention. On the floor between the table and the door, a thick brown folder was splayed open. He glanced back at the files that had toppled from the desk. The stray folder sat another ten feet or so from the rest. Could it have slid all the way there?

Bree and Wesley came up behind Neil, to see what had hap-pened. Neil pointed at the folder near the table. "Was that here when you came in?" he asked his sister.

Blank-faced, Bree shook her head.

Neil glanced around, making sure no one was hiding under the table waiting to grab his ankle. Bending down, he examined the folder. He read the name on the tab. "Rebecca Smith?" He stood and held the folder out so they all could look at it. He flipped through several pages, which appeared to be doctors' notes, test results, medication forms.

Finally, Wesley spoke up. "We came here looking for answers. I think someone just gave us a whole bunch."

CHAPTER
THIRTY-SIX

WHEN THEY GOT BACK TO THE AUNTS' HOUSE, Bree ran upstairs ahead of the boys to change out of the white dress she'd put on that morning. It had gotten dirty during the impromptu excursion.

Luckily, Claire and Anna were still distracted in the barn. Sounds of the Grateful Dead blasted out from the workshop. Neil felt a pang of guilt as he strolled by the open door. Maybe they weren't the best custodians, or caretakers, or whatever people wanted to call them, but he knew the aunts cared.

Carrying the file, Neil and Wesley came around to the front porch, where they lay their prize open between them. Bree sat down beside him before he'd turned a single page.

Maybe all she'd needed were further hard facts and fewer frightening visions. Maybe he saw their mom somewhere in all this mess. Either way, her new attitude gave Neil hope that they'd made the right decision in going back to Graylock.

"Look," said Wesley, pointing at the top sheet. "Her name, birthday, and the date of her admission to the hospital."

Neil reached out and turned the page. "And more. Much more."

Some pages were clearly missing from the file. Others were stained, water-damaged to the point of illegibility. But there was still a lot of information to take in. As they sat and read, time swallowed the afternoon. The life of Rebecca Smith filled their heads.

According to the file, Rebecca had been seventeen years old when she first came to Graylock with severe depression. She'd asked to be admitted to the youth ward because she thought she'd be safe there — safe from whom, she didn't say, but the doctors inferred she'd be safe from herself.

What little information the doctors were able to get from Rebecca revealed that her childhood had been fairly normal, unremarkable. Then, at fifteen, Rebecca's mother was hit by a car while walking on the side of the road. After the funeral, Rebecca'd found herself unable to eat, unable to sleep. When she woke in the morning, she would be overcome by a sense of panic that something horrible was going to happen. Within weeks, Rebecca had slipped far away, into her head.

At Graylock, Rebecca eventually began to socialize with some of the other patients in the youth ward. After a few months, the staff claimed she might even benefit from being released. For Rebecca, this news was devastating. She withdrew into her bedroom — number 13 — rarely coming out except for meals and meetings, during which she refused to speak.

"That's the room we got stuck in," said Bree, her voice quavering.

"It's her," Neil whispered. "Rebecca's our ghost."

"Exactly," said Wesley, shaking his head in disbelief. "So what was wrong? If she was getting better, why didn't Rebecca want to leave Graylock?"

"Maybe she was scared of what she might do to herself," said Bree.

"Or maybe she was scared of what someone else might do to her," Neil whispered.

"Look here," said Wesley, peeking ahead to the last of the pages. "It turned out that Graylock wasn't the safest place for her after all. She died there. She *was* one of the girls who drowned in the lake. This file proves it."

The three of them looked over the copy of the coroner's report.

Bree covered her mouth and closed her eyes. "She was only a little older than me."

The front door swung inward, and the three of them jumped. Neil swiftly closed the folder and sat on it.

"Hey, there," said Claire, from behind the screen door. "Whatcha been up to?"

"Not much," said Neil. "Just hanging out."

Claire bit the inside of her mouth, as if she didn't like that answer. "Anyone up for a trip to Rooster's Drive-In? I don't know about you all, but I'm hungry enough for a hot dog or two. My treat."

Neil and Bree glanced at each other, silently questioning whether they had time for a break.

"They have go-carts," said Wesley, as if that might seal the deal.

CHAPTER
THIRTY-SEVEN

AFTER A GREASY DINNER OF HOT DOGS AND FRENCH FRIES, they all raced go-carts, taking the curves slowly so that none of them vomited. The aunts dared Neil to wallop them, but even after a few trips around the track, he couldn't stop thinking of Graylock. It was as if Rebecca was sitting next to him, pulling at the steering wheel.

When the group returned to the aunts' house, the sun was starting to set. With his bike helmet strapped on tightly and his lips pressed shut in a knowing smile, Wesley took off for home.

A message waited on the answering machine in the foyer — the red light blinking from the console like a stop signal at a crossroad. When Neil heard his father's voice blaring from the speaker, he closed his eyes. "Hey, guys, sorry to miss you again," said Rick. "I've got a big surprise that I'm sure will make you very happy. I'm busy tonight, but we'll talk in a couple days. Love to you all."

Click.

The aunts sighed and went into the living room, giving Neil and Bree privacy in the foyer. "You want to call him back?" asked Neil.

Bree shook her head. Her eyes glinted darkly, almost regretfully. "But there is someone I think we should try reaching out to." Bree grabbed the cordless phone and dialed Information. "I'm looking for a phone number in Heaverhill, New York," she said to the operator, "a nursing home called Whispering Knoll."

Mrs. Reilly had been there on the night Rebecca had drowned. They both agreed that they needed to ask her about it.

Neil dialed the number Bree had written down. The phone rang once, twice, three times. He was about to hang up, when a voice said, "Good evening. Whispering Knoll. How can I help you?" Neil asked to be connected to Mrs. Reilly's room. After some hesitation, the receptionist, told him to hold.

After nearly a minute, a male voice came on the line. "Who is this?"

Neil recognized Mrs. Reilly's son. He didn't sound happy. "Um . . . My name is Neil Cady. I met you yesterday —"

As if he'd been waiting for the call, Nicholas interrupted. "My mother has nothing more to say to you. And if you keep bothering us, you're going to be very sorry. Do you understand me?"

Neil nearly dropped the phone. All the breath exited his lungs. "I . . ."

The line went dead, and moments later, a dial tone rang in his ear. Neil put the phone back in the cradle.

Bree leaned forward, eyes like flying saucers. "What happened? What did she say?"

"*He* said I was going to be very sorry." Neil shook his head. "I don't think we should call there again."

CHAPTER
THIRTY-EIGHT

LATER, UPSTAIRS, NEIL AND BREE SAT ON HIS BED, discouraged, flipping through the pages of Rebecca Smith's file.

"I still can't believe Nurse Janet's son," said Bree. "So weird."

"Yeah," said Neil, unsure if *weird* was the right word for what Nicholas Reilly actually was. "I don't know. I keep thinking about the way he watched us when we went up to Whispering Knoll, like he wanted us to disappear or something."

"He's trying to protect his mom," said Bree, distractedly turning another page of the folder, landing on a blood-test report. She glanced up at Neil. "He doesn't want her to have to deal with anymore Nurse Janet questions."

Something popped into Neil's head, something he hadn't considered before. "Maybe he's hiding something."

Bree flinched. "Like what?"

"Mrs. Reilly could have lied," said Neil, sitting back against the pillows near his headboard. "If Nicholas knew that, what would he do to keep anyone from learning what really happened at Graylock Hall?"

Bree pulled nervously on her hair. "You don't think . . ." She exhaled slowly, evenly.

But for Neil, the room spun. "I don't know," he choked out. Nicholas's voice stuck in his head like caramel. He tried to remember his dream from the other night, to make out the face behind the flashlight chasing him through the woods. Could it have been Mrs. Reilly after all? Maybe she actually *was* crazy. And maybe it ran in the family. "I wish Rebecca could just tell us what to do!"

Neil felt a chill. He glanced around the room. There was no breeze, and yet he was suddenly cold. Bree rubbed at her arms. The papers lying between them fluttered a bit. Neil and Bree both looked down, bringing their hands away from the folder. Something on the page caught his attention.

"Bree," Neil whispered, "look." He pointed at a name typed near the top of the document: DR. JULIUS SIMON.

According to the hospital record, the doctor who had ordered Rebecca's tests was the same one who'd bandaged Neil's leg. Neil drew back from the folder, as if it might suddenly slam shut on his hand.

CHAPTER
THIRTY-NINE

THE NEXT MORNING WAS COLD AND GRAY. A white mist filled the usually sunny spaces between the trees that surrounded the Victorian house in the woods. When Neil woke and glanced out his bedroom window, he imagined momentarily that the fog was a mass of apparitions congregating in the shadows, waiting to descend upon him. Vague memories of bad dreams stuck in his head like cobwebs in a long-forgotten attic.

Coming downstairs, a name flashed in his brain, shucking away the last remnants of sleep: Julius Simon. Neil had suggested the night before that they reach out to the doctor today. Bree, however, was still on the fence about it. He might be dangerous, she argued. Neil was thankful to find the rest of his makeshift family sitting at the kitchen table. Claire asked Neil and Bree if they wouldn't mind helping out at the register, since Lyle called out sick. The two quickly shared a look — being in town would bring them closer to the doctor's office. But was that a good thing?

By the time they got to the shop, the morning rush had already passed — Melissa Diaz had been able to cover until they arrived. Claire taught Neil and Bree how to ring up the customers, then went back to her office.

Even with a steady trickle of customers, though, Neil couldn't stop thinking about Dr. Simon. Rebecca had obviously wanted them to find her file. But did she wish them to visit the doctor? Or avoid him at all costs? Either way, Dr. Simon was the only clue they had left.

Returning to the front after a bathroom break, Neil tapped his sister's shoulder. She screamed and spun around, her hand raised up as if ready to smack him. He flinched. "Whoa there," he said. "Jumpy?"

Bree closed her eyes and shook her head. "You wouldn't believe what just happened." Neil raised his eyebrows. "I was standing here, counting out the last customer's change, when I looked up and noticed a car parked across the street. Guess who?" Neil shook his head. "Nicholas Reilly."

They both went out to the sidewalk, but the car that Bree had seen was gone. The roads were damp and fog obscured the distance.

"How sure are you that it was him?" Neil asked.

"Pretty sure," said Bree. "His eyes were shooting bullets." Neil didn't care for the expression. After all, what might the man do to protect his mother? "Going up to Heaverhill was a big mistake. We've got to tell Aunt Claire and Aunt Anna what we did. If Mrs. Reilly's son is here in Hedston, he could hurt us. He could hurt *them*."

Neil knew she was right. The aunts needed to know everything. But if he told them now, they might stop him from talking to the doctor, and he wasn't ready to give up his biggest lead, especially since Rebecca had practically handed it to him. "Please don't say anything," Neil said, stepping away from the door of the pie shop, heading down the street. "Not yet."

"Neil," Bree said, her voice raising like a warning alarm. "Where do you think you're going?"

"Someone has to help Rebecca," said Neil, beginning to run.

"But what about *us*?" Bree called back.

Same thing, Neil thought. His sneakers slipped on the sidewalk as he turned at the corner. Catching himself before he fell, he looked ahead into the mists that swirled between the houses, trying to remember the way to Dr. Simon's office.

CHAPTER
FORTY

AFTER A FEW BLOCKS, Neil came to an intersection that looked familiar. The sign at the corner read Yarrow Street. Several driveways down, the white building sat back from the road, a small sign crookedly pitched in the middle of the lawn: DR. JULIUS SIMON — FAMILY MEDICINE.

During his frantic run, Neil's mind had been spinning — had Nicholas Reilly followed him? Was Rebecca watching? If he didn't do what she wanted, would she barrage him with the dangerous visions again?

Now that he faced the long walk up to the doctor's front door, reality began to solidify around him. He would ask Dr. Simon about Graylock. About Rebecca.

He pressed the doorbell and waited. A few moments later, the knob turned and the doctor's mother, Maude, opened the door. She wore the same floor-length white nightgown she'd had on the last time he'd seen her. Her outfit struck Neil as odd, reminding him of what he'd once imagined was Nurse Janet's uniform, of Rebecca Smith's own white hospital gown. Could Maude's clothing be a clue? Everything seemed to mean something now.

Neil blinked at the old woman. She scowled. "Mrs. Simon," he blurted out. "Hi. I'm Neil Cady. I was here a couple days ago."

"I remember," she said, reaching out both arms to grasp the door frame, blocking the way. Her son must have told her about the folder he'd confiscated from Eric. She obviously didn't trust him now. "How's your leg?"

"Actually," Neil said, thinking quickly, "that's why I'm here." This was his in. "Do you think Dr. Simon could take a look at it?"

"Why?" said Maude. The old woman was as tough as she looked.

"Pins and needles," Neil answered, standing his ground. "It hurts."

"Have you been cleaning the wound?" She crossed her arms. "I believe that Dr. Simon gave you all the instruction you required." As she leaned toward him, Neil realized how tall this woman was. He imagined her reaching out for him, pushing him down, her long fingers closing around his throat.

Then another thought sparked his imagination: If this woman's son had once been a doctor at Graylock Hall, was it possible that she'd worked there too? Had she known Nurse Janet . . . or Nicholas Reilly? Was Maude as frightening as she appeared to be, or was she simply annoyed that he'd disturbed her?

Neil stepped back, forcing himself to speak. "I've been trying." His voice came out like a whisper. He cleared his throat and tried again. "But I really wanted to talk to Dr. Simon about it."

Maude shook her head violently, as if she might send him forcibly away simply by thinking about it.

Neil gritted his teeth. Rebecca would be angry if he didn't get inside. And the longer he stood here, the better chance Nicholas had of tracking him down — if he hadn't already done so. Neil steadied himself, ready to attempt a dash past Maude, when a voice called from the darkness inside the house. "Who is it, Mother?"

Maude stepped aside, revealing her son standing at the end of the long hallway, in the entrance to the waiting room. "Neil?" said Dr. Simon, stepping forward. "What's wrong?"

Neil knew that this was the last chance he'd have to turn and walk back to the relative safety of the pie shop, to meet up with what was sure to be a furious Bree. He paused in the damp air just outside the open door. Then, slowly, trying to stop the shaking he felt in his bones, Neil stepped over the threshold and into the blue hall, past the woman who glared down at him with eyes like acid.

"Dr. Simon," he said, "please, I need your help."

CHAPTER
FORTY-ONE

THE WHITE ROOM WAS EVEN MORE CRAMPED than Neil remembered. Tall, freestanding exam lights were shoved into the corners; stainless steel containers filled with Band-Aids, Q-tips, and syringes were crowded on the countertop. A big red bin labeled BIOHAZARD sat on the floor next to a wide wooden desk. Neil perched once more on the paper-covered table as Dr. Simon sat on the stool by his feet, looking closely at Neil's shin. After a few seconds, the doctor glanced up. "You could have kept it covered for another day or two, but it looks like it's healing just fine without a bandage," he said. "It still hurts?"

"A little," said Neil, clutching at both sides of the exam table. He worried that the doctor's mother was listening from the other side of the door. But he knew that the longer he kept up the story of his leg bothering him, the harder it would be to spit out the real reason he'd come.

"I'd recommend ibuprofen. I'm sure your aunts —"

"Do you remember Rebecca Smith?" Dr. Simon stood up, surprised. He tilted his head in confusion, as if he hadn't heard Neil correctly. Neil forced himself to continue. "She was a patient of yours a long time ago." Dr. Simon stared at him, his puzzlement seeping away, replaced by what looked like frustration.

"If you know that, then you already know my answer," said Dr. Simon.

Neil took a deep breath and crossed his ankles. He tried to imagine what Bree might have asked if she'd had the guts to tag along. "Can you tell me anything about her?" he tried.

"I'm sorry," said Dr. Simon. "I can't talk about my other patients."

Neil thought quickly. "Can you tell me about working at Graylock Hall?"

The doctor glanced at the door, as if contemplating walking out. "I moved to Hedston to be one of the general medicine physicians at Graylock," he said in a rush. "I took care of many patients. Some of them got well. Some of them did not. Everyone knows it was not a nice place, but we did the best we could under the circumstances. When they shut Graylock down, I decided to open a private practice here in town. Mother and I have lived on Yarrow Street ever since."

Leaning forward, Neil asked, "Did your mom work with you?" When the doctor stepped closer toward the door, Neil tried a different question. "Did you know all the patients who drowned?"

Dr. Simon blinked. "What do you know about Rebecca Smith?" he asked.

"I know she died at Graylock Hall," Neil heard himself say. "I know she drowned in the lake."

"Do you really?" Dr. Simon's mouth seemed to twist into a slight smile. "And how do you know that?"

Neil needed to make Dr. Simon understand how serious he was, so he said, "She told me."

Dr. Simon's mouth dropped open momentarily before he clicked it purposefully shut again, holding onto that strange, forced smile. "She told you," he said with a look of condescension. "Of course she did. And what else did she *tell* you?"

Here it was. The big question. Neil closed his eyes. "She said she was murdered."

"Ah, yes." Dr. Simon nodded as if this suddenly all made sense. "You've heard the stories." He chuckled. "You *do* know that Janet Reilly lives north of here? She's a lovely woman. We were friends once."

"Nurse Janet wouldn't hurt anyone?" asked Neil.

The doctor shook his head. After a few seconds, he said, "So who do you think did it? Who *murdered* Rebecca Smith?"

The ghost stories of Graylock Hall had twisted so many times in the past few days, Neil was having a hard time keeping everything straight. He knew he could probably come up with a list of suspects if he thought hard about it. Nurse Janet, who everyone believed had been the killer, was now an old woman, but her son, Nicholas, certainly seemed like a threat. Dr. Simon hadn't answered Neil's question about Maude working at the hospital with him, but did that mean that his mother might be guilty of murder? And then there was Dr. Simon himself. Several days ago, he'd confiscated Eric's folder. He may have been the one who'd told the aunts about their first trip to Graylock Hall. And now, he wore that strange smile. Was he merely amused at Neil's persistence? Or did his expression hint at something darker?

Neil tensed up. Talking about Rebecca had brought attention to himself. If the murderer was still out there, he or she wouldn't be happy that he was asking questions. But what else was he supposed to do? Sit in a closet? Hide away?

Dr. Simon stepped close to the exam table — his eyes glinting with an icy intensity — and placed his warm hand on Neil's shoulder. "Did Rebecca mention that she was terrified of the dark?" the doctor asked, his voice low, severe. "Or that lightning storms sent her into a total panic? Did she say how she'd never learned to swim?" Neil listened in silence as the doctor went on. "Did she tell you how very easy it was to slip out of the hospital? To get lost in the reeds? To mistakenly wander into the water?" Neil leaned away, trying to get out of the doctor's grip. "What happened to those kids at Graylock Hall was an accident. Horrible. Tragic. Unforgettable for those of us who were there. But an accident, nonetheless. The last thing this town needs is for rumors of *murder* to surface again. I'm sure Rebecca's family would appreciate a moratorium on the subject."

"Rebecca's family?" said Neil, sliding off the table. "They're in Hedston?"

Dr. Simon flinched, realizing he'd said too much. "I think it's time for you to go."

But Neil's feet felt glued to the floor. If this news wasn't exactly what he'd come for, it certainly sounded like a worthy clue. "Did Rebecca Smith *grow up* here?"

Dr. Simon's face turned red as moved to the exit — his blush was as close to an answer as Neil'd be getting. The doctor grappled with the door, swinging it inward before stumbling, exasperated, into the waiting room. "Mother?" he called. "Can you please show our patient out?"

CHAPTER
FORTY-TWO

THE HIKE BACK TO THE SHOP WAS DAMP AND CHILLY. Neil stuck to backyards and alleyways. Every time a car passed by, a jolt of nerves rocked his bones.

When Neil walked through the shop door, he braced himself. Claire would surely be waiting for him with a worried look. He was certain his sister had told her everything.

But the shop was quiet.

Bree stood behind the register, glaring at him as he tentatively stepped toward her. "Did you find what you were looking for?" she asked.

"I didn't know what I was looking for," said Neil. "But I definitely found *something*." Bree chewed at the inside of her lip, curious but unwilling to ask him what he meant. "Did you tell Aunt Claire what's going on? Are we in trouble now?" Bree shook her head, but she still glared at him. Even if she hadn't ratted him out, she wasn't looking happy about it. "I thought —"

"I thought I would too," said Bree. "After you took off, I came back in here and went to the office. But before I knocked on the door, I felt as though someone was beside me. When I turned, though, no one was there."

"Rebecca?" Neil asked.

Bree ignored his question. "I heard that voice again. It was so quiet, I'm not sure if it was in my head. It said, 'No.'"

"No?"

"That's all. And I suddenly knew I couldn't tell Aunt Claire. For whatever reason, that little *No* got me. I came back out here feeling someone walking behind me, nearly stepping on my heels. I've been waiting for you ever since." She exhaled. "So what happened? What did you find?"

Neil told Bree everything, including Dr. Simon's accidental hint that Rebecca Smith had lived in Hedston and that her family might still be here too. She didn't look happy when Neil suggested they try to track the family down.

"Remember that voice you heard in your head?" Neil asked. "It might only have been your own."

Bree sighed, tucking her hair behind her ears. "So look her up, then," she said.

But Neil's Internet search in Claire's office didn't show any Smiths in Hedston. "There has to be another way," said Neil, returning to the front counter few minutes later.

"Well, apparently Rebecca doesn't want us to ask the aunts," said Bree. "So that's out."

Neil nodded even as he considered the precariousness of taking advice from a ghost. "We know other people in Hedston besides the aunts, though. Wesley's family has been here for years. Maybe they can give us some answers."

CHAPTER
FORTY-THREE

AFTER A LONG CONVERSATION WITH WESLEY, Neil hung up the shop's phone and explained the new plan to his sister. It was complicated, but she complimented him on his resourcefulness.

Later, as Claire dropped the two of them off at the address Wesley had given Neil, she smiled. "I'm glad you're doing this. I think it will be good for you two. I've always wished I could have joined a band when I was your age."

"It's just a tryout," said Bree, opening the passenger door, grasping the handle of her viola case.

"You sure you don't need a ride home?" asked Claire, looking more hopeful than he'd ever seen her.

Neil opened his door too, feeling a heavy blanket of guilt. He promised himself he'd tell the aunts *everything* sometime soon, no matter the consequences. "Eric said he'd drive us when we're done."

"Try to be back before dark. And call us before you get on the road." She might as well have said, *No long joyrides, please.* "I don't want Anna to worry."

"We will," said Neil, stepping onto the sidewalk, pushing the door shut.

Claire honked the horn as she pulled away.

Neil cringed, glancing up the hill.

The Diazes' house sat at the top of a large green lawn. Two stories tall and five windows wide, it was bigger than most of the other houses in Hedston. Painted gray, the building nearly blended into the fog. Bloodred shutters flanked each window, standing out like wounds.

Neil looked around for Eric's car, but the only vehicle nearby was the one parked halfway up the house's long driveway. It was a small, familiar-looking red hatchback. This was the car that had passed them a couple days ago during the walk to the library. According to Eric, Bobby Phelps — the jerk who'd shouted at them — would be here.

The hatchback made everything concrete — there were no ghost stories here, no haunted hospital, no town legends, no nightmares. Neil's goal was real. He was about to face real people. The possibility of real fists. *Real pain.*

From behind Neil and Bree, the sound of tires on wet pavement came up the street. They turned to find Mrs. Baptiste's car pull to the curb. A moment later, Eric and Wesley stepped out, wearing worried expressions.

"Wesley filled me in," said Eric, pocketing his mother's keys. "Sorry my parents weren't any help." He smiled. "But at least now we've got a chance for some awesome payback."

"You're sure you believe all this ghost stuff now?" Bree asked.

"Whatever." Eric shrugged and flashed a well-practiced grin. "Either way, I'm happy to be of service, especially if it gets me back in your good graces." Bree looked at the ground and tightened her grip on the viola's case.

"You guys ready?" Wesley added.

"Well, I've never snuck into someone's house while they were still in it before," said Neil. "But there's a first time for everything. Right?"

They all slowly hiked up the driveway.

"I'm not sure how much time you two will have," Eric said to Neil and Wesley. "Me and Bree might get kicked out immediately, so you'll need to get upstairs as quickly as possible. Melissa's old room is the first door on the left, facing the back of the house."

Neil interrupted. "Her mother's high school yearbooks are on a bookshelf there?"

"Mixed in with Melissa's own." Eric nodded. "I remember flipping through them one night. Every year is labeled on the spine. Grab the earliest ones. According to the dates you found in her file, I'm pretty this Rebecca girl was in Mrs. Diaz's class. The yearbooks will definitely have some sort of dirt on her."

As they came closer to the garage, a loud drumbeat echoed out across the otherwise quiet neighborhood. Eric nodded at Neil and Wesley, then pointed toward the backyard. He had to raise his voice slightly so they could hear him. "The patio door is always unlocked. Head straight through the kitchen. Stairs are on the left." The boys nodded. Turning to Bree, Eric said, "Ready to impress them with your skills?"

"I hope so," Bree said, holding up her case. She looked slightly green. "I'm supposed to be your new girlfriend, right?"

Eric nodded. "Melissa's brother, Tony, was mad when he found out that she'd been hanging out with me again. That's the reason they kicked me out. If I'm with *you* now, I'm hoping they'll let me back in . . . at least for a few minutes."

"I thought you said you quit," Wesley said quietly.

Eric scowled. "Same difference. I'm not *really* trying to get back in. I'm just trying to help you guys figure out this ghost nonsense."

"So we'll be acting, then?" said Bree.

"Sure," he said, amused.

"And they're not expecting us?"

Eric shook his head. "I've known about this rehearsal since last week . . . when everything went down."

"How serious *are* you and I, exactly?" Bree asked him. "Like, are we in love?"

"We're as serious as it takes for these two to get in and get out fast and safe." He swatted at Wesley's hair.

"I still don't understand why I couldn't have just asked Melissa for the yearbook myself," said Neil. "She likes me."

"Don't be too sure," said Eric. "Yes, Melissa wants to keep her job at Claire's shop. But that doesn't mean she'd help out, especially not the brother of the 'new girl' in town."

Bree flinched. "She's jealous of me?"

Eric stared at her for several seconds, then nodded. "Pretty much." Bree looked as if she wanted to smile but knew she shouldn't.

"One more question," said Neil, trying to squash the awkward feeling that had risen up among all of them. "What happens if Wesley and I get caught?"

Eric glanced at the red hatchback parked behind them, his face growing serious. Bobby Phelps's catcall — *Two freaks and a geek!* — seemed to hum silently in the quiet fog as the drumbeat inside the garage grew louder and faster. "Let's not think about that," Eric said, taking Bree's free hand and stepping toward the wide-open door.

CHAPTER
FORTY-FOUR

As Bree and Eric disappeared into the garage, Neil and Wesley were able to sneak around to the back of the house.

Inside the patio doors, a colorful glass lampshade hung over the kitchen table. It cast a mystical glow into the yard where the two boys stood.

Neil yanked the door handle. It slid open. The muffled drumbeat stopped abruptly. Wesley's eyes went wide, and he looked as if he might turn and run. After a few seconds, Neil tugged on Wesley's ratty sweater, dragging him into the quiet kitchen. Muted voices came from behind a closed door on their right. The garage. Neil didn't know what reaction Eric and Bree were getting from the rest of the guys, but that wasn't important. What mattered was the distraction. The staircase was visible through a doorway in the opposite wall. Nodding to Wesley, he crept toward it.

A plush gold carpet covered the stairs and dampened their footsteps. Once Neil reached the upstairs hall, he heard a different kind of sound coming from the garage. No drums. No voices. His sister's strings were singing. That was a relief. They had some time to explore.

The door on their left was closed. Wesley tentatively pushed it open. Bree's viola continued to echo through the house, coating the evening with a soothing sense of safety.

"Is this the right room?" Wesley whispered, peering farther in. After his eyes adjusted to the dim light, Neil glanced in to find a twin-sized bed, dark purple walls covered with posters of rock bands from the '90s, a pile of dirty laundry underneath an open window. Beside a closet door, a tall bookcase was crammed with so many volumes, Neil worried briefly that even if he found the books he was looking for, he'd never be able to squeeze them out.

"Looks like it. Come on." Keeping the light off, Neil headed toward the shelves. Wesley followed closely behind, closing the bedroom door.

Eric had been right. The yearbooks were grouped together on the bottom shelf. There were eight in total. The green, faux-leather spines were pristine, and on them the gold-stamped years seemed to shine almost magically. Neil wiggled the first four books out from the shelf in one clump. "These must have belonged to Mrs. Diaz," he said, handing two of them to Wesley.

They were about to crack the books open when they heard a noise in the hallway — footsteps slowly shuffling against the carpet. Someone was upstairs with them. The boys stood, unsure what to do. Even if the rear window had been a viable escape option, there wasn't time to reach it.

Wesley nudged Neil's arm and nodded at the closet.

CHAPTER
FORTY-FIVE

THEY MOVED SWIFTLY, shutting the door almost completely before they heard a click followed by hinges creaking from across the room. As clothes hangers poked his spine, Neil held his breath and hugged the yearbooks against his chest. The space was small and smelled weird, like a mix of flowers and sweat. He felt Wesley's shoulder against his own. Neither of them said a word. A crack of gray light came in through the slight gap at the closet door.

Footsteps padded deliberately toward them. Neil braced himself as the presence came closer. A dark shape stepped in front of the closet, nearly blocking out the last little bit of light. Neil pressed himself backward into the closet. He heard a gurgling noise beside him. Wesley's stomach. It was no comfort to find his friend panicking too.

The figure continued to stand before the closet, as if trying to make up its mind whether or not to grab the knob and pull.

Neil's head spun as he strained to hear his sister's music. But it wasn't playing any longer. What if Eric and Bree had been forced to give away their plan to the band? What if the guys were furious? What if Bobby Phelps — *two freaks!* — had come upstairs and was standing just on the other side of this door?

Neil's imagination took another leap forward, and placed Nicholas Reilly's face onto the shadowy form outside.

An odd smell wafted inside the closet, different from the one he'd experienced moments ago. This was a moldy, rotten aroma. Plant decay.

Neil's knees buckled.

He knew who was standing out in the bedroom. He felt for Wesley's hand, just to be sure he wasn't alone. The shadowy figure appeared to be staring at them through the gap. Neil couldn't make out any features; it was too dark. The scent grew stronger, and he felt nauseous. The shadows seemed to squeeze at him. His own fear choked the air from his lungs, and that familiar painful feeling crept from his fingertips up his arms.

Rebecca, he thought. *Why are you doing this? We're trying to help you!*

The bedroom light flicked on. A sliver of light burst through the opening at the closet door. The shape that had been standing just outside was gone.

Now, a humming voice entered the room. It was Melissa Diaz.

Again, Neil's stomach dropped.

Through the gap, Neil watched Melissa plop down on the bed and kick off her shoes. He figured she wouldn't be so peppy if she knew that Eric and Bree had arrived together — she clearly wasn't in on band practice. She reached over and turned on her clock radio. Pop music burbled out from the tinny speaker. She sang along, stretched and yawned, looking as if she was settling in for a while.

Neil's mind raced, trying to think of some way he and Wesley might be able to get out, or at least signal to Bree that they were stuck. Then another thought came along and stomped on his foot — what if Bree and Eric had assumed that he and Wesley had made it out without a problem? What if they'd simply left?

The closet door creaked open several inches, and Melissa stopped singing. Neil clenched his jaw, ready to smack Wesley for even thinking about touching the door. But when he turned to look at his friend, Wesley shook his head slightly. He hadn't been near it.

If neither of them had moved, and Melissa was still on the bed, then Neil knew only one other person could have tugged on the knob.

Please, Rebecca, he thought. *Don't!*

"Tony?" Melissa said, her voice trembling. "Is that you?" She sat up as the closet door opened another couple of inches. Neil had to squeeze closer to Wesley so that she wouldn't see him. "This isn't funny."

Across the room, the door to the hallway slammed open and Melissa screamed. Neil and Wesley couldn't see what she was seeing. "Who's there?" she shouted.

Wesley whispered in Neil's ear. "What the heck is going on?"

"It has to be Rebecca."

Seconds later, Neil watched as the entire contents of the bookcase tumbled onto the floor in front of the closet with a crash, followed immediately by the case itself. Melissa screamed again. She dashed out of the bedroom and raced quickly down the stairs.

Neil understood what Rebecca had done. She'd known Melissa was coming and had warned them into hiding. Knocking over the bookcase had gotten Melissa out. Rebecca hadn't meant to scare them. She was helping them escape.

"Now!" he said. "Let's go!"

CHAPTER
FORTY-SIX

THE BOYS SHOVED THE CLOSET DOOR against the shelves, pushing forward with all their weight. They squeezed themselves out through the small gap into Melissa's bedroom.

Clutching the yearbooks, Neil and Wesley careened into the hallway and down the stairs. They froze in the foyer, listening to a commotion of voices coming into the kitchen from the garage. Melissa must have alerted her brother and his friends that someone had been upstairs. The bookcase crash had probably shaken the whole house, freaking out everyone even more.

In the foyer, Neil and Wesley spun toward the front door. They yanked it open and darted out into the night, running and sliding across the damp lawn, not slowing until they reached the street. They crouched behind Mrs. Baptiste's car, unsure what to do.

Shouting continued to come from up the hill, louder now than before. Tony and his friends must have discovered the ruins of the bookcase in Melissa's room.

Two shadowy figures exited the garage and dashed down the driveway. One of them was hugging a large case — the viola.

Eric drove, not knowing where they were going. Neil and Wesley peered out the rear window, making sure no one was following them. After several hurried turns, Eric pulled the car to the curb and flicked on the overhead light. Water condensed on the windows, collecting and streaking down the glass.

They were parked on a purgatory street, surrounded by forest, the nearest houses far ahead and behind them. The trees on either side of the road were becoming silhouettes against an already muted sky, the sun still hidden behind thick clouds.

If they didn't head home soon, the aunts might come back to the Diaz house looking for them. Right now, though, Neil knew they had bigger problems.

"Well, the band fell in love with Bree, especially when she started playing," said Eric. Bree shook her head, as if she might be able to wiggle away from her embarrassment. "But what happened with you guys? Melissa burst into the garage, screaming her pants off."

From the backseat, Neil and Wesley recounted their story. Eric and Bree listened with urgent attention.

"Yearbooks," said Eric after they had finished, pointedly ignoring the tale's ghostly aspect. "Brilliant. What gave you the idea to track them down, Neil?"

"Dunno," said Neil. "The idea popped into my head this afternoon when I was on the phone with Wesley. It just came to me — I almost could have sworn a voice had whispered it in my ear. But it definitely wasn't Wesley's voice." Bree shivered and hugged herself. "Anyway, we're just lucky you knew where to find the books we needed, Eric."

"I can't believe we pulled that off," said Wesley. "When it was happening, I wasn't sure we would."

"So . . . if Rebecca wanted you guys to get these yearbooks out of there," Eric said after they'd finished, stealing an uncertain glance at Bree, "there must be something good inside."

"That's what we were hoping," said Neil. The books sat on the seat between him and Wesley. All four of them stared at the pile. "There's one for each of us." He picked them up and handed them out.

Neil held Rebecca's freshman year in his lap. He opened to the class photos section and quickly found her portrait surrounded by those of her classmates. She stared up at him from the page, her eyes as wide as her toothy smile. Her long brown hair was parted down the middle and tucked behind protuberant ears. She glowed with a happiness that made Neil sad.

According to the earliest pictures, Rebecca could have been any girl on the verge of great things — a girl filled with possibility, who saw the world as a treasure chest waiting for her to come and crack it open. Put together, however, the four volumes revealed a different kind of story, one whose morbid ending became more apparent with every page turned. By her senior year the exuberance that had existed in Rebecca's fourteen-year-old face was gone, as was her smile and any hope that it might have contained.

Neil, Wesley, Bree, and Eric spent nearly half an hour sharing the books with one another, flipping through the pages and indexes, looking for a moment — some indication — of where, when, and why things had changed for her.

"Wait a second," said Bree, after she'd gotten hold of Rebecca's junior year. "Here's something strange." She lifted the book so they all could see. Near the front, a photo of a woman filled nearly half a page. A name was printed beneath the photograph — Mrs. Alice Curtain. Mrs. Curtain had brown hair cut into a bob. She wore large glasses, a reserved smile, and a pink twin-piece sweater set. She looked off as if she'd been caught unprepared for the shutter to close. At the top of the page were the words *In Memoriam*.

The principal had written a brief eulogy about Alice, about how much the town would miss her, about the good work she had done at the school. He proclaimed that the accident that had caused her passing was a tragedy and should act as a reminder that every day must be seen as a gift.

"She died earlier that year," said Bree.

"Who was she?" asked Wesley.

"Duh," said Eric. "She was obviously a teacher."

"Yes," said Bree, "but she was more than that." She pointed at what looked like a short poem at the very bottom of the page.

> *For My Mother*
> *"Do you remember the way home?" she always asks, like*
> *A woman in a fairy tale protecting her*
> *Daughter from the*
> *Dangers of the world.*
> *"Yes," I remind her*
> *Dutifully, as*
> *I step into the woods, haunted by*
> *Desire for certainty and her dread. I promise to leave a trail*
> *of clues*

In the dark, for her or me or someone who follows.
The bread crumbs glow. None of us are alone.
— *Rebecca Smith*

"Alice Curtain wasn't just *any* teacher," Bree continued, her face drawn, her skin pale beneath the car's overhead light. "She was also Rebecca's mom."

CHAPTER
FORTY-SEVEN

By the time Eric had driven Neil and Bree back to the aunts' house, the wind had picked up and lightning flashed in the distance. The sun had gone down, and the front porch light was on, straining to cast its orange glow through the thick mist and increasingly strong rain.

Turning into the driveway, Eric sighed. "Will Claire and Anna be mad that you're late?"

"We'll be fine," said Neil, his voice hushed by doubt. He gathered the yearbooks from the backseat and opened the car door. "But we have to find out some more about Mrs. Curtain. Learning what happened to her will give us a clue about what happened to her daughter. These must be the glowing bread crumbs Rebecca left behind." He thought of her poem. *"A trail of clues in the dark,"* he said, wearing a bleak smile. "Let's talk tomorrow. Okay?"

Everyone nodded, their exhaustion weighing heavily on them. As Bree got out of the car, grappling with her case, Wesley slipped past her into the front seat. Before she closed the door, Eric leaned across him, calling out the window. "Hey, Bree," he said, "you really do play a mean violin. Those guys would be lucky to have you in their band."

Bree smiled crookedly. "Thanks," she said. "Same to you." Neil noticed with amusement that she hadn't corrected him — she played viola, not violin.

A growl of thunder rolled by overhead as Eric drove off.

Neil and Bree dashed across the lawn toward the front porch and up the steps. Before she could reach for the door, Neil grabbed her arm. "Wait," he said, nearly dropping the four books as he glanced back at the driveway. "Look." Two vehicles were parked there instead of the usual one. The aunts' Chevy sat closest to the barn. Behind it, a black minivan seemed to slumber. "Isn't that Mom's car?"

The front door swung inward. From behind the screen door, a tall figure stood in silhouette, staring out at Neil and Bree. "Well, look who finally made it back," said a deep voice.

Neil's body went instantly numb. He hadn't heard the voice in such a long time, his instincts told him he must be dreaming. He shivered — the cold water that soaked his shirt seeped into his skin. He realized, unfortunately, that he was awake.

Bree stepped forward, a strange smile plastered across her face. "Dad?" Her voice was unnaturally high and shook like a child who was on the verge of tears. "What are you doing here?"

CHAPTER
FORTY-EIGHT

INSIDE, NEIL AND BREE SAT ON THE COUCH in the living room as their father leaned against the fireplace mantel and told them his story. Claire and Anna listened from the kitchen — this was the second time they'd heard him go through it that evening. From the looks on their faces, Neil knew they couldn't stomach it again.

California hadn't worked out, he explained. The casting agent had broken every promise she'd made. He said that he'd come back to New Jersey mostly because he missed his family, and he knew they'd welcome him home.

"This afternoon," said their father, "I flew into Newark, I took a cab back to the house, and borrowed your mom's car. I drove all the way up here for you guys." He grinned, as if he'd just presented them with an enormous, brightly wrapped gift. "You can pack your things. We'll leave tonight. Whaddaya say?"

Neil wished he could squeeze himself backward into the couch hard enough that it would swallow him up. He couldn't look at his father's face — determination and hope combining into an expression that filled Neil with nausea.

"What does Mom think?" Bree asked. The little girl with the wavering voice was gone.

A chip of the gleam fell from Rick's smile. "We'll surprise her."

Neil found himself shaking his head. "No," he said. "I'm not leaving."

Now Rick's smile crumbled entirely. "We'll be together again," he said, stepping toward his children. "Come on. Don't be like that. Bree, can't you talk some sense into your brother?"

Bree seemed to choke on her thoughts. Then she said, "If you knew Neil at all, you'd understand that sometimes he *doesn't make sense*. I certainly don't have the power to change his mind, and I doubt you do either." She turned and smiled weakly at Neil, and he knew that she hadn't meant to insult him. What Bree had said was true, and she seemed proud of him for it. "Maybe if you'd been around for the past few months, you'd have seen that."

Rick turned red. "Well, you guys might not have a choice." He crossed his arms. "After everything your aunts have told me, I'm not sure how much longer they'd like to keep you around."

Anna came from the kitchen and stood in the doorway. "I can tell you the answer to that one," she said. "Bree and Neil are welcome to stay as long as they want to."

Neil's face burned with surprise. Was that true? Had his fears about being sent away only been in his head? Maybe. Maybe not. Either way, his father's appearance had galvanized the aunts against him.

Rick scoffed. "I appreciate the offer," he said, "but I think we'll pass."

"It's more complicated than that," said Claire, joining Anna in the door. "Linda may still need some time to herself. Did it even occur to you to ask her what she wants? Just because you've decided to come home doesn't mean we're all ready to have you back."

Anna sighed. She took Claire by the arm and led her around the corner into the hallway.

Rick was left alone in the living room with Neil and Bree. "Thanks a lot," he whispered, his tan face looking sunburned and suddenly old.

"I'm sorry, Dad," said Bree, reaching out for his hand. But he stepped away. Then, to Neil's horror, she added, "We'll think about it, okay?"

A moment later, Claire and Anna came back into the room. Anna nodded toward the front door. "Come on, Rick," she said. "Let's go for a ride."

"A ride? Where?"

"We need to talk in private," said Claire, glancing briefly at Neil and Bree. "You can take Anna and me to dinner."

"What about us?" Neil asked, standing up.

"There's some food on the stove for you two," said Anna. Neil hadn't been asking about dinner, but he kept his mouth shut. "Help yourselves. We won't be long."

Annoyed, Rick shook his head as he grabbed his car keys from his jacket pocket. He glanced at his children. "Go pack your things," he said again. He turned and followed the aunts out the front door.

CHAPTER
FORTY-NINE

THE MINIVAN STARTED UP WITH A ROAR. The headlights shined momentarily through the living room windows before the car backed out of the driveway, its tires spinning on the slick road as their father gunned the engine.

Seconds later, Neil and Bree were alone.

They stood in the foyer, staring at the door as if it might burst open again, all three adults laughing and patting each other's shoulders, proclaiming how funny a joke the last fifteen minutes had been. But that didn't happen. The rain only came down harder, raising a din of white noise that threatened to drown out the sound of Neil's own thoughts. Glancing at his sister, he forced himself not to speak, because he knew if he did, the words would be, *This is what you wanted. Right?*

"What do we do?" she asked, almost as if to herself. "Should we pack?"

Neil shook his head. "I'm not going anywhere with him. At least not until Aunt Claire and Aunt Anna kick us out."

In the living room, he slid over the top of the couch and landed with a *whoomp* on the cushions. The stack of yearbooks that had been sitting there toppled to the floor. Rebecca's junior year landed open to the page remembering her mother.

Bree stood behind him, looking at the book from over his shoulder. "I suppose we need to decide which are more important right now: the problems of the living or the problems of the dead." She came around and sat down. Picking up the remote control, she turned on the television. "I honestly don't want to think about either."

An old black-and-white movie was on. Neither of them recognized the actors, but Bree didn't change the channel. She seemed to stare right through the screen, as if she was seeing something Neil could not.

Neil picked up the yearbook from the floor and examined Alice Curtain's portrait again. He read over Rebecca's poem several times, the strange words seeming to slowly seep into his skull.

Why did Alice have a different last name? he wondered. She must have married a man who was not Rebecca's father. The incomplete Graylock file had left so many questions unanswered. How frustrating that she wasn't able to just appear and tell him, forced instead to use subtle hints and partial clues.

Glowing bread crumbs.

Ever since he and his sister had entered room 13, it seemed that these clues had lead them down a dark, secret stairwell, one that no one had traversed in a very long time. Why them? Was it because they lived so close to Graylock Hall? Or maybe one needed a certain kind of awareness to recognize mysteries hidden in plain sight. Despite the horror of the past year, what had happened between Neil's mother and father may have allowed him and his sister to understand the world in a way others did not. Like how Wesley noticed Green Men in ordinary hillsides, Neil and Bree had been forced to see the world in a different way. Maybe this was the reason Rebecca was drawn to them. Maybe this was why she'd taken them to the lake and shown them her death.

Glowing bread crumbs.

But no, Neil thought. She hadn't given them nightmares to merely make them aware that she'd died. Or even to learn that she'd been murdered. She wanted them to do something for her. She needed them to see the clues she'd left behind. She knew that, because of their mom, they'd be more likely than most to help.

Looking into the yearbook, Neil's heart felt as if it stopped. The poem. It had suddenly changed shape. The biggest clue yet stared directly up at him. His hands trembled as he lifted the book to show his sister. "Look," he said. "She left a message."

When Bree noticed how pale Neil had become, she grabbed the book from his hands, then reached out and smoothed his hair away from his forehead. "What's wrong?"

"The first letter in every line of Rebecca's poem," Neil managed to say. "Read them straight down."

Bree concentrated on the page. She recited the poem aloud.

"Do you remember the way home?" she always asks, like
A woman in a fairy tale protecting her
Daughter from the
Dangers of the world.
"Yes," I remind her
Dutifully, as
I step into the woods, haunted by
Desire for certainty and her dread. I promise to leave a trail of
    clues
In the dark, for her or me or someone who follows.
The bread crumbs glow. None of us are alone."

A look of horror blossomed across her face, and her mouth fell open in shock.

"*Daddy did it*," she whispered.

CHAPTER
FIFTY

THERE WAS A FLASH OF LIGHT, a crash of thunder, and the room went suddenly dark.

They both screamed, then moved so quickly toward each other on the couch that they nearly bumped heads. It took them several seconds to realize what had happened. The storm had knocked the power out.

Neil glanced around the room, but he couldn't see much. Rain continued to pound the roof. Lightning flashed again, briefly revealing tree branches outside, whipping about in a strong wind. Several seconds later, the house shook under the crushing sound of thunder. Neil pulled his knees up to his chest and hugged himself. Thunderstorms didn't usually bother him, but on top of everything else . . . this one was a nightmare.

He felt the yearbook poking into his leg. He swatted it away, and it fell to the floor with a loud slap. "Rebecca Smith died on a night like this."

"I wish we had cell phones," said Bree, as if deliberately trying to not think about the ghost story they were living.

Neil took his sister's hand. "Bree," he said, "we know who killed her. She wrote it in the yearbook."

Bree was quiet for a few seconds, then nodded. "She wanted everyone to know, but was too scared to tell."

"That's why she looked so different from her sophomore to

junior year," said Neil. "Like two different girls." *Shadow people.* "What causes that?"

"Fear."

"If she knew her mother had been murdered by her father, maybe she was afraid that she'd be next."

"Yeah. She might have been right. Especially if her father thought she might tell someone."

"She *did* tell," said Neil. "But did he find out?"

"Maybe," said Bree. "Maybe not. We know she went into Graylock afterward. Her doctors said she was crazy, but was she really?"

"You think she was pretending?" Neil asked.

"Maybe she thought she'd be safe in there."

"But she wasn't safer. He tracked her down."

"He knew where she was. He was her father."

"And since they lived here in Hedston, he must have also known that several patients had drowned in that lake," said Neil. "Drowned on nights like this, when the power went out and that back door unlocked automatically. Rebecca hadn't considered that. On the night she died, her father knew that if he got her out of the building, he could make her death look like an accident. Another tragic drowning. And she'd never attempt to tell what he'd done to her mother again like she had in the yearbook."

"So horrible," Bree whispered.

Neil and Bree stared at each other for several seconds, their eyes growing accustomed to the darkness. The wind howled through the eaves above. The wood creaked, sounding as though someone were walking around in the attic. Bree glanced at the ceiling. "I really wish we could call someone."

"We'll be fine until the aunts come home," said Neil, trying to reassure himself.

"And then what?" Bree asked, finding her voice again. "We pack our things and leave with Dad?"

"We can't! We need to find Rebecca's father."

"But he's a *killer*, Neil," Bree whispered. The television flickered blue light. Static came across the screen. "Hey, look," she said, relieved. "The electricity's back."

But the rest of the house remained dark. Only the television seemed to be working.

"I don't think so," said Neil nervously.

Together, they watched as a fuzzy image came into focus through the grainy TV snow. Soon, the picture was sharp, clear, and vividly bright: a pair of antlers hanging from a wood-paneled wall. "Oh no," said Bree. The image shifted, showing a piano bench piled high with sheet music. Neil knew that the next would be the fireplace with the white birch logs piled on the andirons.

But no. The final image was different this time. When the white logs appeared, Neil noticed that they were spattered with drops of a dark red liquid.

Blood.

CHAPTER
FIFTY-ONE

NEIL STOOD, HIS ENTIRE BODY TINGLING WITH GOOSEFLESH. "Did you see that?" He pointed at the television, but the image had changed. The antlers again.

"Which part?" said Bree, standing too, taking his hand. The piano bench flickered by again. And finally, the third image answered her question. She gasped when she noticed the spatter, then glanced at Neil. "What does it mean?"

Neil didn't answer. He didn't know.

The three pictures flashed by repeatedly, faster and faster, until they became a blur not much different than the static out of which they'd appeared. The screen turned bright white and then black. Again, they were tossed into darkness, unprepared.

The front door slammed open. The wind rushed into the foyer.

Bree screamed. Neil dashed around the couch, catching the handle and pushing with all his might until the latch had clicked shut. He flipped the dead bolt.

"How did that happen?" asked Bree, a high voice in the shadows of the living room. Neil knew her real question: Had someone opened the door?

In the dining room, the floor creaked. They turned toward the noise.

"Who's there?" Neil asked. But of course, no one answered.

"Neil," said Bree, making her way to the foyer, "I really don't like this."

"Well, I'm having a blast," Neil said. Bree's lip trembled and he immediately hugged her, feeling bad for the joke. "Do you want to wait for everyone outside? On the porch?"

In response, the brightest lightning bolt yet struck just across the street, followed by an explosion that seemed loud enough to break eardrums. The two leapt away from the door, tripped, and tumbled to the floor near the bottom of the stairs.

Blinded, Neil blinked the flash out of his eyes and tapped at his temples until he was certain he still had all of his senses.

Another creak came from down the hallway. This one sounded closer.

Silently, Bree waved at Neil, then pointed at the stairs.

Was she really suggesting they go hide up there? He raised his eyebrows in an expression that asked, *Are you nuts?* "We'd be trapped," he whispered.

Then a deep voice called softly from the other room.

"*Rebecca . . . ?*" The voice sounded far away and close at the same time. "*Come here, sweetheart.*"

Bree clutched at Neil's hand, crushing his fingers against the floor. They froze as another footstep fell closer still.

Was Rebecca's father a ghost too? The idea seemed suddenly plausible. Their Internet search hadn't turned up any local Smiths — and there would be no Smiths left in Hedston if they were all deceased.

How badly had this man wished to keep his secret? *Ghosts can't hurt you*, Neil thought. *Baloney.* Rebecca had hurt them many times. But was it possible for the dead to silence the living completely?

Neil's mind ran laps around the room. His eyes fell upon the cordless phone that sat on the sideboard against the wall. But the connection light was out. With no power, that phone would be as useless as a cell. They needed a phone that plugged directly into the wall. A landline. He thought he remembered seeing one out in Anna's studio.

In the barn.

"Rebecca . . . ," the voice called once more. *"You're safe now. Come out, darling."*

Another footstep creaked on a floorboard around the corner of the staircase.

"Rebecca . . . ?"

Any closer and he'd be upon them.

CHAPTER
FIFTY-TWO

NEIL SEIZED HIS SISTER'S HAND so hard that she cried out. He stood, dragging her to her feet.

"What are you —" Bree started to ask, but Neil dashed toward the front door, pulling her behind him.

Outside, the rain was coming down so ferociously, it hurt as it hit them. As Neil flew around the corner of the house toward the driveway, he realized that it wasn't merely water falling from the sky, but hail as well. Chunks of ice as big as cherries bounced off the asphalt path that led to the studio. The dark shadow of the barn rose up before them. Neil nearly slipped and fell, but caught himself just in time. He prayed that the door was unlocked. Bree cried out from behind him as she too struggled to stay on her feet.

Neil turned to see if she was okay. At that moment, another flash lit the night. Back by the house, a dark silhouette stood. Tall. Rigid. A solid mass of shadow. Mixed with the thunder, his voice rose up in the night.

"REBECCA!!!"

Neil swallowed the panic rising from his stomach. They had to reach the phone in the barn. The building was still a dozen yards ahead. He pushed himself to run faster than he ever had before. He stumbled over the icy obstacles covering the driveway. One large lump fell from the high roof of the barn and struck his cheek, just below his eye. "OWW!" he cried.

The world went white — lightning or pain? But there was no time to stop.

As Neil reached for the doorknob, a flash of foliage appeared around him. He was suddenly enveloped by the tall, thin reeds of Graylock Lake. He remembered what Rebecca had felt in the dream — the terror of being chased, the knowledge that one slip could cost her life. And did. For just a moment, he was there, *he was her*, and the shadow behind him was reaching for his neck. Ready to grab, to shove, to push down and hold him underneath the surface of the freezing water —

Cold, wet metal filled his palm. Neil clutched the knob and turned. He shoved the door open as Bree crashed into him from behind, knocking the two of them to the floor once more. Turning over, Neil kicked at the door. It slammed shut.

They were alone in the barn.

Anna's desk was on the far side of the room. Once there, Neil tried to flick on the desk lamp, but the barn had no power either. *Focus*, he told himself. Then he saw the phone sitting in its cradle on the other end of the desk. When Neil held the receiver to his ear, he cried out in joy. The dial tone buzzed musically, calmly, as if trying to assure him that everything was going to be okay.

Bree came up beside him, stammering. "I saw . . . I saw the swamp. Just now. I was there. Her father was coming for me."

"I saw it too," said Neil, turning the receiver over, looking for the glow of the push-button keypad. "He brought us there. Just like Rebecca did in our dreams."

"But how? Why?"

"I don't know!" said Neil. Exasperated, he spun toward his sister. "Who am I calling?"

"The aunts?" she said, her voice wobbly with panic. "Dad?"

"No cell phone service. You know that."

"Call the police!"

"And tell them what? That a murderous ghost is chasing us? That we learned he killed his daughter and now he's coming for us too?"

"I don't know! Call Wesley. Call Eric. Anyone!"

"By the time they get here —" Something loud crashed out on the driveway. Neil craned his head to see through the window of the barn door, but the night gave no clue who or what was out there. He imagined a face staring back at them, cloaked in pitch, his smile growing wide, the rain mixing with blood and saliva as it ran down his chattering chin.

Neil groaned, a cramp stabbing his side. His cheek felt warm where the piece of hail had hit him. Bree shook her head and closed her eyes. Her own face was wet. Rain. Tears. Neil couldn't be sure, but he knew just how she felt. Helpless.

"Wait a second," he said. He shoved his hand into his pocket, praying silently that he was wearing the shorts he'd had on the other day. His fingers closed upon a small scrap of paper. Yes! He pulled out the scrap, unfolded it, and glanced at the smeared name scribbled there.

Andy

Neil handed the paper to Bree. "Quick," he said. "Read me the phone number."

CHAPTER
FIFTY-THREE

THEY REMAINED HUDDLED UNDERNEATH ANNA'S DESK until a flash of light streaked across the studio's wall. Not lightning this time. An engine rumbled all the way up the driveway. Andy's headlights shined blindingly through the window in the barn door.

Neil and Bree sprinted outside. The rain had begun to let up. Standing next to his truck, Andy opened his arms and both of them barreled into him. He hugged them tightly as they shivered with both cold and fear. Moments later, he held them at arm's length. "Is he still in the house?" he asked, glancing up.

On the phone, they'd told Andy that they thought someone had broken into the aunts' house — it had been easier than trying to explain everything else.

"We don't know where he went," said Bree.

"Can we please just get out of here?" Neil asked, worried that Rebecca's father was watching from the shadows.

"Maybe I should take a peek inside the house," said Andy, stepping away from the truck. "We don't want the aunts coming home to find some creep waiting for them."

Neil held his sister's hand. "But . . . what if he's waiting for *you*?"

Andy stared at the house, searching for a sign of an intruder. After a few seconds, he sighed and turned back to the truck. "Tell you what, we'll head back to my house and try to reach the aunts from there. Sound like a plan?"

They all squeezed into the front seat. As Neil swung the truck's door shut, he sighed, relieved to be in safety's arms again. Andy reversed toward the road. The barn began to shrink before it disappeared into the rain-swept shadows. The house stood in the darkness beside it, looking forlorn and frightened to be left alone.

Andy turned on the radio. Soothing piano music came from the speakers. "You kids gave me a good scare. This'll be a good story for our next movie night." Neil secretly hoped they'd all make it that far.

As they drove off toward Andy's house, Neil couldn't help but remember that they were heading closer to Graylock. For a moment, he wondered if that was the best idea. But then he glanced in the rearview mirror.

Lightning lit the night, and Neil nearly screamed. Briefly illuminated in the road behind them, the man he'd earlier seen standing in the driveway was running toward them.

Even over the roar of the truck engine, Neil heard his voice calling.

"REBECCA!!!"

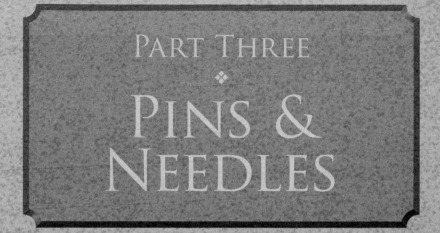

PART THREE

❖

PINS & NEEDLES

CHAPTER
FIFTY-FOUR

LESS THAN FIFTEEN MINUTES LATER, Neil and Bree were sitting in Andy's fully lit kitchen. Luckily, his house hadn't lost electricity. Still, Neil couldn't stop himself from flinching at every random creak or gust of wind. What if the ghost of Rebecca's father had followed them here and was waiting for the perfect moment to burst through the door?

"Would you like some milk? Sugar?" Andy asked, placing two steaming mugs onto the table between Neil and Bree. They usually didn't drink tea, but they nodded anyway, trying to forget about the horror that had chased them into the storm. They huddled in their chairs, wrapped tightly in the warm towels that Andy had taken out of his dryer for them. Outside, the rain had died down, but the soft *pat-pat-pat* of water dripping from branches onto the forest floor echoed in through Andy's screen door.

After he brought a small carton of milk and a cup full of sugar to the table, Andy sat down beside Neil and Bree. "Now," he said, "tell me exactly what happened. I'm not quite sure I understand why you don't want me to call the police."

The two glanced at each other, unsure how to answer.

"It's okay," said Andy, with a concerned smile. "You saw *something*. Trust me. In these woods, you're not alone thinking you might be crazy."

Crazy . . .

"We're not sure what we saw," said Neil. "But it was scary."

"I can tell." Andy leaned forward onto his elbows and clasped his hands, resting his chin on his fists, mashing his beard. "Now why do you think someone would want to break into your aunts' house?"

"We don't actually think someone would want to do that." Neil clasped the hot mug, warming his fingers. "You said you've seen *crazy* things in these woods?" Andy squinted at him. Neil proceeded carefully. "What if we told you that the person in the driveway wasn't quite . . . alive?"

Bree sat up straight, eyes wide, silently asking him what he thought he was doing. But Neil was determined. Andy might have the answers they'd been searching for; they should've talked to him sooner.

"It was a *ghost* chasing you?" Andy smirked. "Or a zombie? Maybe a vampire?" Seeing their horrified expressions, his bald head flushed red. "I'm sorry," he said, trying to sound sincere.

Neil glanced at the clock near the stove in the corner. He didn't know when the aunts would return to the house, but he figured they had some time. At this point, what choice did he have?

Neil told Andy everything he could remember: the figure in room 13, the nightly visitations, the dreams, the strange pictures on the camera. He even mentioned their trip up to Whispering Knoll, and Nicholas Reilly's reaction. Neil revealed the truth about Rebecca Smith's death, about reading her clue in the yearbook, about how her father's ghost had come for them, Neil theorized, to stop them from revealing his secret to anyone else.

As he spoke, Neil felt a weight lift from his shoulders. Now he and Bree weren't alone. Andy looked concerned. And that was a relief. If Neil and Bree were forced to leave Hedston that night, at least someone knew what had happened at Graylock Hall. Maybe Rebecca would find the peace she so desperately sought.

"That's . . . quite a story," said Andy, shaking his head, keeping his eyes on them.

"You believe us, don't you?" Bree asked.

"How could I not? It all adds up. Remarkable, actually." Then, to their surprise, Andy chuckled. "You two should write a book!"

Bree glanced at Neil. "Maybe we will," she said, hesitating, "someday."

"But first," said Neil, "we've got to figure out who Rebecca's father was."

Bree sucked her teeth. "What I want to know is how to stop him from coming after us again."

"We could get in touch with the *Ghostly Investigators*," said Neil. Bree scoffed.

Andy chuckled, pushing his chair back. "That is one question I definitely cannot answer for you." He crossed around the table and headed through a darkened doorway and down a short hall. "But we can try and look him up on my computer," he called out.

Neil and Bree followed him, leaving the towels draped on their chairs in the kitchen. Stepping into the darkness of the hall, they heard what sounded like a soft cry. The noise gave Neil chills. Feeling foolish, he closed his eyes, then walked faster toward the light and the comfort of Andy.

When Neil entered the room, he realized that the sound hadn't been a cry, but merely the plinking of piano keys. The large instrument stood against the far wall beside a rain-spattered window. Andy had his back to them, moving papers off a desk and opening a laptop computer. His hip brushed against the piano again.

Plink. Plink. Plink-plink.

Neil sighed. His mind was still filled with Rebecca's story. He needed to stop, to take a deep breath. To —

Bree grabbed his hand so suddenly, Neil nearly screamed. When he tried to pull away, he caught a glimpse of her face, and it froze him solid. Her eyes were wide, her lips pressed together so tightly that the skin around them was white. Cords of muscle stood out from her neck, and, for a moment, Neil wondered if she was having a seizure. But then Bree flicked her eyes toward the wall behind him. She shook her head slightly, with a quiet violence, as if to say *Not. A. Word.*

Slowly, Neil turned.

His body went numb, his eyes completely dry. He clenched his jaw and didn't even blink when he tasted the blood he'd drawn from his tongue. He felt as though the entire world was spinning too quickly — at any moment, gravity would stop holding him down. He'd hit the ceiling and that would be it. And maybe, right now, that would be for the best.

Above the stone fireplace, hanging from the dark, wood-paneled walls, a pair of deer antlers appeared to be reaching for him — sharp little skewers that could poke out his eyes if he got too close. Below the mantelpiece, in the mouth of the fireplace pit, a pair of black andirons held up three white logs. Neil knew it was birch wood. He'd seen them several times before — pictures of them, at least.

Neil turned away from the fireplace as quickly as he could.

Andy threw him a strange glance, as if he suspected the terri-fied thoughts rushing through their heads. "What's the matter?" he asked. "You look like you've seen . . ." He chuckled. "Aw, heck, I'll say it. You look like you've seen a ghost."

"Nope," said Bree, forcing her voice into an unnatural-sounding calmness. "No ghosts. Still a little freaked-out from before. That's all." She let go of Neil's hand and stepped back toward the door. "You know, maybe my aunts are home now. Can we use your phone?"

"Of course," said Andy, nonplussed. He gestured to a small table next to the piano bench, where his phone sat. Neil trembled when he saw a large pile of sheet music stacked on the bench, on top of which lay "Superstition" by Stevie Wonder. Neil squeezed his fists to keep himself from shaking. Andy rose and stood between them and the door. "Anna's probably dying of worry." He leaned against the wall and watched them expectantly.

Neil noticed a framed document hanging on the wall at Andy's shoulder — a certificate of commendation from the local Kiwanis club. A name leapt out from the center of the frame.

ANDREW CURTAIN

Curtain? It was Alice's last name . . . Rebecca's mother.

But how? Neil wondered frantically. *We saw the killer's ghost back at the aunts' house.*

Andy noticed the alarm written on Neil's face and turned to see what had caught his attention. As he studied the certificate, his concerned expression transformed, looking both happy and sad, as if he had resigned himself to a difficult task.

After a few seconds, he spoke. "Rebecca was never my daughter," he said. Bree dropped the phone receiver and turned around. "But her mother *was* my wife. Our relationship was . . . complicated, but eventually the girl did learn to think of me as her father."

Daddy . . .

Andy reached down and allowed his hand to brush against the iron fireplace instruments: a brush, a shovel, a pair of tongs. But the piece he ended up wrapping his fingers around was longer, heavier, and sharper than the rest. The fireplace poker had a hooked tip. "Unfortunately, that didn't last very long," he said, stepping quickly toward them, his boots falling heavy against the hardwood floor.

CHAPTER
FIFTY-FIVE

THE ROOM FLICKERED AND, for a moment, a series of images flashed through Neil's mind.

Andy stood in a different position, closer to the fireplace. He was shouting, towering over the woman from the yearbook memorial — Alice Curtain, his wife and Rebecca's mother. Behind Andy, in the doorway, Rebecca cowered, an iron mask of terror locked upon her face.

Then Alice was lying on the floor, her hair matted with blood. On the way down, she'd hit her head on the andirons — the white birch logs were now spattered with red. "Momma!" Rebecca screamed.

Andy focused on the girl, swaying as if he was having a difficult time staying on his feet. Neil understood that the man had been drinking. "It was an accident," Andy said, wide-eyed, guilt oozing from his lips.

"You pushed her!" Rebecca raced past him to cradle her mother's head in her lap. "Momma, wake up," she pleaded. "Please! Wake up."

Andy gripped Rebecca's bicep, her skin at his fingertips turning white. She peered up at him with a look of hatred and fear, but said nothing more.

When Andy spoke, his voice was low. *"She slipped."*

Neil knew instantly that there existed a different kind of haunting than those he'd seen on television with Alexi and Mark. Here was the ghost of Rebecca's memory.

She'd sent him all those pictures — the antlers, the piano bench, the birch logs — because she'd needed him to enter this room. The energy was powerful here. She was using it to tell him the rest of her story, just as she'd used the electricity from the aunts' house to try to show Neil and Bree who had chased her through the reeds at Graylock Lake. Neil recognized now that what he and Bree experienced earlier that night had not been the ghost of Rebecca's father coming for them but the memory of her last moments on earth. She'd been trying to reveal his identity.

The visions continued —

Andy bringing Alice's body out to the road, calling the police himself to report a hit and run . . .

Andy visiting Rebecca in her room late at night after everything was over. *Promise me you won't tell . . .*

Rebecca only staring back at him, her eyes wide with fear, keeping her mouth shut, as if that was what he needed to see in order for him to believe her.

"Who else knows about this?" Andy stood before them, clutching the fireplace poker like a police baton. "You mentioned your friends Eric and Wesley. What about Anna and Claire?"

"No one knows anything," Bree answered quickly, backing up against the couch.

Andy cocked his head. "What did you think would happen when you started digging around? That you'd learn the truth about

Rebecca, and everything would be fine afterward? You'd go back to your life in New Jersey?" he said venomously. "Who cares what happens to the folks up here in Hedston — the ones who had to deal with all this nonsense the first time around. Right?"

Against all better judgment, Neil opened his mouth. "So we were supposed to close our eyes? Ignore what we were seeing?"

"Why not? It's what everyone else did." Andy's eyes sparked with lightning fury. A moment later, surprisingly, he seemed to let it go. He sighed. "None of this was supposed to happen." Neil agreed silently. "Rebecca was a troubled girl," Andy said, sounding full of regret. "More than anyone knew. But I loved her. You have no idea what she was capable of. The manipulation. When I found out about that poem in the yearbook, my heart almost stopped.

"She practically begged them to put her away in that place, though why she'd want to be locked up is beyond me. It was an insane request. Maybe the doctors were right. She was very sick."

Bree spoke up. "You think Rebecca made it all up?"

"Oh, I'm sure she *believed* that I was guilty for all the bad things that happened to our family. But it's only natural for children to blame their parents for their own problems." This last sentence was like a knife to Neil's gut, as if Andy had meant for it to hurt. He'd flung it so casually. Heartlessly. "Come on." Andy nodded toward the door. "I'll drive you home."

Bree flinched. "You will?"

Andy sniffed, offended. "Your family is probably worried to death. Do you have another suggestion?"

Bree quickly shook her head. "No, sir."

❖

Outside, Neil marched silently next to Bree as Andy followed behind them dragging the poker through the dirt.

Neil did not believe they were going home. If Andy had intended to let them go, why had he brought the fireplace poker with him?

Maybe he'd simply forgotten he was holding it.

Andy had figured out what Rebecca had written in the yearbook. *Daddy did it.* That could have been what had tightened the screw. He'd come for her at Graylock during that long-ago storm to stop her from talking again. If he had no qualms disposing of his own stepdaughter, then what were his neighbors' niece and nephew worth when it came to maintaining his illusion of innocence?

Unless he was being truthful and Rebecca had lied. Or maybe she'd gotten it wrong. Maybe she *was* confused, in life and in death?

Neil was kicking himself for not leaving a note before they'd left the house earlier that night. But then he wondered if a note would only have put the aunts and their father in danger when they inevitably came knocking on Andy's door.

If Andy was innocent, he'd let them go. If not . . . they had to run. Now.

Neil grabbed his sister's hand. Together they dashed into the wet bushes at the edge of the driveway, the darkness of the woods swallowing them whole.

CHAPTER
FIFTY-SIX

THEY RAN, NEARLY BLIND. Mud and muck and leaves stuck to their clothes, creating a natural camouflage.

An occasional remnant of lightning lit the sky. The night made the seemingly endless woods treacherous. Low branches and tree roots reached out from both above and below trying to ensnarl them, as if nature itself were hungry for the taste of their blood. Still, the more distance Neil put between himself and Andy's house, the better he felt.

Somewhere behind them, Andy called out. His deep bellow was familiar. Rebecca had remembered the sound of it for them back at the aunts' house. Moments later, the truck's engine rolled over, then groaned to life.

"The roads will be the first place he'll look," said Bree, struggling to catch her breath.

They splashed upon wet ground. Water soaked their ankles. The sky lit up once more, and the island shined through the trees in the distance, its dark building appearing like a slumbering monster. The gravel path extended from the entrance and into the trees like a slobbering tongue.

"Once we reach the bridge," Neil whispered, "we'll find the way home through the woods."

They circled around the edge of the lake, following the tall reeds that marked where the deeper water began. They listened closely to the sounds of the forest, rain dripping from leaves, the wind creaking branches above them. As Neil trudged along, he waited for the telltale sound of Andy's boots splashing through the flood plain, but it never came.

When they were about halfway to the concrete bridge, he asked his sister if she'd shared the visions Rebecca had shown him in Andy's parlor.

"It was so weird," she answered, nodding. "It all happened so fast. Like a dream." She wiped at her face. "I don't understand *why*."

"What do you mean?" Neil asked.

"I mean: *Why* would Rebecca show us all that and then leave us alone to deal with him?" Her voice quavered, growing almost too loud to be discreet. She caught herself and, whispering once more, added, "Is she trying to get us killed?"

Neil flinched. He hadn't considered that.

Bree had said it herself a few days ago: Ghost stories were always sad. If Rebecca was lonely, what might she do to change that, to keep a couple of new friends to herself up here in Hedston? What if the visions she'd been sending them hadn't merely been messages? What if her bread crumbs were meant to lead them directly into the wolf's den? If so, her plan had worked so far.

"We can't think about that right now," said Neil. "Let's get home."

After hiking up a small incline, they reached the gravel path that led to the hospital. Beyond the chain-link fence that sagged across the path on their left, Graylock Hall waited, as if it had been expecting them to return for a permanent stay.

Shivering with a chill that went beyond dampness, beyond cold, Neil pointed across the road, deeper into the woods. "This way."

Bree grabbed his arm. "What was that?"

Just then, a pair of headlights flashed on, blinding them. Several hundred feet to their right, Andy's truck sat with its engine off.

Neil and Bree froze, unsure which way to go. With the lights illuminating a good portion of the forest, Andy would see whatever direction they ran. Any way they went, he'd be on them within seconds.

Neil thought about that sharp hook at the end of Andy's fireplace poker. Out of the corner of his eye, he watched Bree shudder. He suddenly had an idea — a *dangerous* idea, but it might have been their only option. "Come on," he said. "If we make it to the water, we can swim out. Hide on the other side of the lake until we're sure he's gone."

"What about the weeds? Isn't that how Rebecca —"

"We'll just have to be careful," he interrupted. Bree groaned in protest. "We have no choice!"

Up the road, the truck's engine roared to life, and the headlights lurched forward.

CHAPTER
FIFTY-SEVEN

NEIL AND BREE LEAPT OFF THE ROAD and scurried down the incline, bypassing the chain-link fence, which towered high on the threshold of the bridge above them. When they reached the reeds in the shadows at the water's edge, the bright lights went out and the engine died with a whimper. Somewhere in the darkness, they heard Andy curse — he obviously hadn't meant for the truck to lose power.

The reeds were thick. Neil and Bree had to push hard through them. Mud sucked at their feet, trying unsuccessfully to hold them in place. Carefully, they made their way into the bog. The first wall of greenery closed behind them, hiding them from the possibility of Andy seeing them in the water.

Up on the road, they heard the truck door open. Footfalls scattered stones across the path. A crunching sound came down the incline toward the water's edge. Andy had seen them descend.

Neil and Bree forced themselves forward, the water growing deeper, lapping at their waists now. Lily pads swirled all around them, long stalks entangling their legs. With every step, Neil found it harder to move. Just ahead of him, Bree bent down, trying to pull the plants away from her body.

Briefly, Neil imagined gray hands emerging from the water, grabbing his sister, and dragging her under. He quickly blinked the thought away.

Coming down this way was a mistake. There was no way they'd make it past this barrier toward the open water. They should have taken their chances back in the forest.

A loud whooshing noise slashed at the air behind them. Andy was using the poker to break through the reeds.

Straining forward, Neil couldn't help but imagine how strange it would be to die in the same way as Rebecca. Remembering his frightening dreams, Neil thought with an odd giddiness, *At least I already know what it'll feel like.* Pins, needles, and infinite darkness.

"Neil," Bree whispered, bringing him back to reality, "I can't." She was stuck, her hands trapped below the surface.

"No," he insisted, pushing at her shoulders. "Don't stop." To his horror, Neil watched Bree sway forward under his touch, rippling the water's lily pad cover, as her feet sank in the muck.

But at the last moment, just before her head went under, something strange happened. Bree wrenched her arms up in front of herself and then jerked forward several feet toward Graylock Island. Neil saw his sister land with a groan on the steep shore. If he didn't know better, he'd have thought someone had pulled his sister to safety.

Another whack of the reeds came from close by. Andy was making his way quickly through the water behind him.

Neil tried to pick up his feet, but the harder he heaved, the more the mud sucked on his sneakers, as if it wanted him to stay put.

Something brushed his face. It felt soft. Fleshy. Neil nearly screamed. Then he heard a voice in his ear. "*Shh.*"

A dim shape appeared before him, reaching out as if from inside an impossible pocket of darkness near the shore. Five delicate fingers wavered slightly. A hand. It came closer. Neil gasped. When another splash sounded from the water behind him, he instinctively took hold of it.

A sharp, icy cold enclosed his wrist with surprising strength. Neil felt his breath being stolen from his lungs. Before he knew it, he was lying on the beach.

Speechless, Bree grabbed his arms and helped him to his feet. Dizzy with confusion, they sprinted up the small embankment together and found themselves standing amidst the rows of tall pines that lined the rocky path to the hospital.

Another slicing sound came from the water at the base of the bridge. Another curse. Andy was nearly at the opposite side of the small channel.

"Which way?" Bree said to Neil, glancing back toward the chain-link fence. Imagining what might happen if they got caught in its teeth, Neil shook his head.

Everything that happened that week had led to this moment, this decision whether or not to seek refuge in the empty asylum, to enter its shadows and hide from the man who had killed Rebecca Smith.

The ghost had wanted this to happen.

But, Neil wondered as he reluctantly turned with Bree to face Graylock Hall, *can we trust her?*

CHAPTER
FIFTY-EIGHT

GRAVEL AND DIRT SPAT UP FROM THEIR SHOES as they splashed through sodden ground. Their wet clothes clung to their skin. The hailstones had mostly melted, and the sky that had created them was almost clear. A bright-white half-moon was coming up over the horizon ahead. Neil and Bree raced along the side of the building, past the boarded-up window where they'd first entered the hospital, toward the shattered patio at the other end of the island. Their ears pounded with sounds of their own making, so that by the time they reached that broken back door, they were both unsure if Andy had heard where they'd gone.

Standing on the concrete among the invasive weeds, Neil grabbed the handle of the door to the youth ward, feeling both panic and relief when it turned. Pulling the door open with a nearly imperceptible slowness, he managed to dampen the possibility of squealing hinges until he'd opened a wide-enough gap for Bree to squeeze through. He followed her briskly onto the platform just inside, then just as slowly as before, he closed the door, wishing there was a way to lock it.

All they had left was a slight hope that they'd been quiet enough to escape. They only needed to hide in here until they were sure that Andy had given up. Gone home.

And then what?

Neil knew Andy wouldn't stop there. What about Wesley and Eric? What about the aunts? No. He and Bree couldn't merely hide. They needed to get back. To warn everyone else. To tell them what they'd learned.

Someone was walking outside the door. Heavy boots kicked gravel.

Neil's heart sank. He imagined that fireplace poker reaching out for the doorknob, the hook catching hold.

Neil held the inside handle as tightly as he could, his palms slipping over the smooth metal. The door rattled. Bree took hold of the handle as well, leaning backward with all her weight. But it wasn't enough. The door creaked slowly outward.

Through the slight crack that appeared, Andy peeked in at them. His eyes were wide, lifeless. Practically robotic. The man had a mission. He would not be talked out of it. Raising his top lip in a canine grimace, Andy threw his shoulder backward, yanking the door even farther open. Neil and Bree strained with every ounce of strength to simply hold on, and somehow, they managed to keep their feet just inside the jamb.

"I can't," said Bree, her strength fading.

"Let go," Neil whispered. "On three." He nodded and they released the door.

Andy stumbled backward.

They had only seconds to run.

The staircase led up to the youth ward's common room and down to the mysterious depths of the boiler room. It wasn't even a choice which direction they'd take.

At the top step, Neil and Bree slammed themselves against the cage gate. It swung wide and hit the wall. Behind them, the outside door yawned open too. Neil reached out and shut the cage as Andy burst through the entry onto the platform at the bottom of the stairwell. He glanced up at them, clutching the poker in both hands. Then he came, taking steps two at a time.

Bree dragged Neil to the other side of the cage just as Andy used the hook to smack the mesh door open. Andy pulled himself into the common room, swinging around the corner as Neil and Bree clambered to the opposite side and the stairwell leading to the bedrooms above.

They slammed this next gate shut, but it swung open again, refusing to catch. Andy approached, chortling a wheeze of triumph. Bree paused at the bottom step, her fingers sticking through the small diamond-shaped openings in the wires, trying to latch the cage door before Andy could work it open again.

Andy raised his hook and slammed it against the metal. Bree screamed and pulled her fingers out of the way as the mesh was crushed. But the latch held. When Andy tried to pull the door open again, it caught with a jolt. He'd smashed the cage so hard, the crushed metal had blossomed inward, creating a makeshift lock, putting a barrier between himself and his target. Realizing his error, Andy released a howl of anger that echoed through the room.

Neil wanted to sneer, to stick out his tongue or worse, but Bree was already halfway up the stairs, calling for him to follow her. When Neil turned back, he found that the common room was empty. Andy had already gone.

CHAPTER
FIFTY-NINE

UPSTAIRS, BLOCKS OF BLUE MOONLIGHT spilled through the open bedroom doors, illuminating the otherwise pitch-black corridor. Bree and Neil stood at the beginning of the hall, glancing back and forth between the direction they'd come and the darkness they knew they would find ahead. Bree held Neil's hand, and he felt very young. He thought he could feel her heartbeat pulsing in her fingertips. If this had been some other place, some other time, he would have pulled away. Left her alone. Maybe even made fun of her. But here, he understood that inside that thrumming feeling, that beating beneath their skin, the same blood flowed through their veins. He knew he needed her. Now and for the rest of their lives — however long that happened to be.

Wind battered the building, and something knocked against the nearby windows. Twigs, leaves. Remnants of the storm. Bree squeezed his fingers even tighter.

"It's just how we left it," Neil whispered. It was something to say. His voice sounded funny up here. Lonely. Loud.

From down the stairs, a clanging noise echoed through the common room. "He's looking for another way up," Bree said. "We have to get out of here."

Neil glanced down the stairs at the busted mesh gate. "But the door's stuck."

Releasing a measured sigh, Bree stepped into a puddle of moonlight that shimmered out from the closest room. "Then we need to look for another way *down*."

At the end of the hall, they turned the corner and met a wall of darkness.

Stepping lightly, noiselessly, they passed the point where Neil was certain they'd first encountered Rebecca Smith. Room 13. The shadows here were so dark, they almost seemed to be filled with color, in the way strange shapes sometimes appear behind your eyelids if you press on them. *Where was Rebecca now?* he wondered. Was she watching them? She'd pulled them from the lake, but did that mean she was on their side, or did she simply wish that they'd die *here* instead?

They felt their way along the walls to another bend. Another double doorway. Another hall.

"What do you think happened back there?" Neil whispered as they blindly continued on. "At the aunts' house? When we heard Andy calling Rebecca's name?"

"It wasn't Andy, obviously," said Bree after several seconds and several footsteps. "It was Rebecca's memory. Wasn't it? I mean, that's what's been haunting us all this time. Andy's voice, his apparition, was just another part of it. What I don't get is why would Rebecca reveal that part only now? What's so different about tonight than any other night we've been here?"

"Dad came to bring us home," said Neil. "If Rebecca's ghost has been learning how to show herself to us, to tell us the truth about what happened here at Graylock, then she might have had a reason to blast us with everything she had." They'd come to another part of the hallway, lined with windows. For the moment, they could see each other.

"Yeah!" said Bree, stepping quickly past a long-forgotten wheelchair shoved against the wall. "Maybe Rebecca needed the storm and all of the electricity to reveal who killed her."

"But we never saw his face," said Neil. "She *didn't* reveal who killed her."

"Sure she did. She got us to call Andy. She knew we'd find her clues at his house. The antlers, the piano bench, and the birch logs."

"She set us up," said Neil, wishing he could stay where he stood, in the light of the moon. But the darkness of the hall ahead seemed to call to him. Forward was their only option.

"Maybe," said Bree, pulling him along. "But maybe not. *She* didn't ask us to tell her father everything we knew."

"Still," Neil whispered, dragging his heels on the rough linoleum, "how were we supposed to know who he was? What he'd done?"

Bree huffed. "It's too late now to worry about that."

"Way too late," said Neil.

He stopped and managed to hold Bree in place. With her arm outstretched, she turned and threw him an irritated glance — bug-eyed, the one she was so good at. "Please," he whispered, his voice sounding as if it belonged to someone else — someone both older and younger than him, as if it were possible to be those two things at once. "Tell me we'll get home okay. That everything is going to be fine." He didn't care if it wasn't true. He just needed to hear her say it.

"I promise," said Bree. Her words were like an impossible glimmer of light in deep water.

When they'd crossed into the new line of shadow, and their eyes adjusted to the darkness again, Bree and Neil found themselves standing in front of another door. Bree nudged it open with her toe. The hinges popped as the door swung against the wall.

Inside, a desk sat against a line of windows that looked out upon thick pine branches. Beyond those, moonlight flicked silver flecks off the surface of the lake.

"Wait a second," said Neil, glancing at the wall next to the desk. He strolled over to it, reached out, and his hand disappeared into a recessed cavity in the stone. "I know where we are." Bree followed, and together, they peered into the opening. There was just enough moonlight to show them several steps spiraling down. "This is the way Eric came that first day, when he found us in the ballroom. These stairs lead all the way down to the basement."

CHAPTER
SIXTY

THE STEPS WERE SLICK, THE STONE WALLS DAMP. Neil left a fingertip trail as he felt his way along, twisting slowly into the depths of the building.

His sister's breath hushed in his ear, a comforting signal. In his blindness, his imagination soon began to buzz. He imagined turning around to find himself alone — what he'd thought had been Bree would turn out to be nothing, or worse . . . *something else*. "You there?" he whispered, to be sure. His voice came out a little too loud. He wished he could catch it as it echoed up and down the stairwell.

"Yes." Bree touched his shoulder and he felt better, even as he wondered where Andy might have gone.

Maybe he'd be waiting for them back at the bridge.

Don't think about that, he told himself as they passed a small landing and continued down.

After another short while, Neil's foot met liquid instead of stone. He splashed up to his knee as he nearly fell face-first into cold water. Somehow in the dark, Bree managed to catch his arm before he toppled over and doused himself completely.

"The storm flooded the basement," Neil said.

"How deep?"

Neil took another step and sank down to his waist. Reaching

forward, he knew that they had several more stairs before the bottom. "Pretty deep. I'm not sure. Do we swim it?"

Bree sighed. "To where? The boarded-up window? Maybe we could use that desk we climbed in on to get back up and out. But how are we supposed to find leverage when half the gym is underwater?"

Neil didn't want to say what he knew they were both thinking. He squeezed his eyes shut, discovering the same blackness there as when they were open. "We have to find another way."

Turning back, they climbed back to the landing. Neil felt for the wall. "This must have been where —" Before he could finish, he managed to knock open the bookshelf door that Eric had come through on that first day. Before them, the old ballroom appeared, lit dimly by the night spilling in through the tall windows.

They stood in the doorway, listening to the silence, alert for any indication that someone was waiting for them here. A breath, a footstep, a rustle of clothing, a shifting of weight. A trickle of water echoed faintly from somewhere nearby, but that was all. The crows that had met them here several days ago had found shelter elsewhere. The two were alone.

Stepping into the room, Neil turned toward the door that he knew was on the far right wall.

"Wait," said Bree. "That just leads back into the maze of corridors."

"But there's no other way," said Neil. "There's the flooded basement or . . ."

But Bree glanced at the windows across the room. His heart fell.

"You want us to jump?" he asked.

"I wouldn't say *want*," Bree answered, stepping farther into the room. "More like *need*. Come on. Don't think about it, or you'll chicken out."

"We could get seriously hurt. It's a long fall."

"Well, we're not safe in here either. Andy could be anywhere right now. I personally don't want to find him waiting for us around some corner."

Neil shuddered. He knew she was right. "Fine. But be careful. I can't carry you home by myself if you break a bone." As if that was the worst that could happen. "And watch out for the floor," he said. "It's weak."

"I remember."

Together, they stepped toward the broken window in the farthest corner, the one beside the giant mantelpiece where the crows had jeered at them. Several panes of glass were shattered but the frame was intact. Even though they were careful to avoid the jagged hole that had tried to claim Neil as its victim, the floor groaned and whined, sounding like a tired child on the verge of a violent temper tantrum. Feeling safe enough near the sill, Bree grounded her feet and pulled up on the wooden sash. But it refused to budge.

"Locked?" asked Neil.

"Stuck, I think."

"Just break the rest of it."

A crash echoed through the room as the far door — the one that led back into the hospital wings — flung open and hit the wall. As Neil and Bree turned, they saw a white streak enter the room and quickly disappear.

"What was that?" said Bree, pressing herself against the frame.

"Shh." Neil waved her quiet. "Listen."

From down the hall, they heard a flurry of footsteps. Someone was running toward them. The sound grew louder as the person barreled along. Even from far away, he managed to shake the floor.

Wham. Wham. Wham. Wham.

Neil and Bree instinctively crouched beside the rolled-up carpet that sat beneath the length of windows. They huddled as close together as they could, trying to shrink, to hide inside darkness.

The sounds, the tremors, stopped.

In the doorway across the room, Andy stood, his chest quickly rising and falling. He was still clutching the hooked poker.

For a moment, Neil was certain that he couldn't see them.

The man stepped forward. "Sorry, kids," Andy said through harsh breath. "Dead end."

CHAPTER
SIXTY-ONE

BUT THEN HE STOOD THERE. There wasn't enough light to see Andy's face, but his crooked posture showed confusion. "I saw you come in here, Bree," he said.

That wasn't us, Neil thought. *You were chasing your dead stepdaughter.*

After several seconds, Andy snorted. He entered the room, his boots heavy on the wood floor. "Ain't too many places to hide in here. You two might as well come out." He took another step. The building creaked.

Neil held his breath as Bree dug her fingers into his arm. If they stood now, would they have time to work the window open and smash apart the rest of the wood frame?

Andy's eyes would soon adjust, and then he'd see them. Crouched in the corner, Neil and Bree were sitting ducks.

Hoping his sister would follow his lead, Neil leaned forward, gathering the strength to stand, to reveal himself. But then, a tiny silver light flickered in the center of the room, and Neil's brain felt as if it turned off. He watched in awe as the light expanded, filling the darkness with a dim glow, until a shape had formed. A whitish silhouette. A girl.

A voice filled the room, sounding at once both distant and close — an echo from a world next to our own. *"Daddy . . . ,"* said

Rebecca. *"Why?"* She lifted her arms toward Andy as if calling him into her embrace.

And then she was gone.

Andy stood frozen halfway across the room. In the dim light that spilled into the room outside, Neil could make out the old man's gaping mouth. "Becks?" he said, his voice high and quavering. "Is that you?" He glanced all around the room, as if she might still be near, listening. "H-how?" he added, as his eyes fell on the mantelpiece. And then to the floor beside it. His expression changed quickly from awe to surprise . . . to anger. He shuddered, shivering off the memory of his stepdaughter as if it were no more than a large cobweb he'd accidentally walked through. *"You."* He was looking right at them now.

Neil stood slowly. "Leave us alone!" he shouted.

Andy came closer. The hook swung at his side. "How did you do that?" he said. "How did you make her voice?"

"We didn't do anything to you," said Bree, coming up beside her brother. "And neither did Rebecca."

Andy glowered, his brow growing even darker. "You don't know anything about her. About us."

"We know plenty. More than most people in this town," said Neil.

"Too bad for you." Andy raised his hand, clutching the fire-place poker like a baseball bat. Then he dashed toward them, his boots shaking the floor dangerously.

Neil turned toward the window. "Bree! Go." He watched as she lifted her foot to kick out what was left of the broken window frame. Just as the wood shattered, something caught his shirt collar. Andy's hook! He felt a ripping pain light his neck ablaze.

The world tipped upside down.

Bree screamed, a siren sound of panic.

Neil landed on his back and briefly glimpsed the ceiling high above him. An immense pressure squeezed at his back, and when he tried to catch air into his lungs, nothing came. He couldn't breathe. Wide-eyed, he struggled to roll over and dislodge the hook from his collar.

Andy lay sprawled out behind him, his leg stuck into the floor. Dazed but determined, Andy reached out for the poker, capturing the handle once more in his fist. He pushed himself away from the floor — a sad but satisfied look in his eyes.

"Neil!" Bree cried. "Get up!"

Neil managed to inhale a minuscule amount of breath. He tried to move, but he felt as though all strength had left his body.

Andy was kneeling now, pulling his leg from the ragged gap. He raised the poker.

Neil closed his eyes. His mind went blank for an instant before filling with noise — his own voice crying, *"No, no, no, no, no!"*

A great cracking sound interrupted his plea. The entire building seemed to shake. The floor tilted. Neil slid forward toward Andy, who'd lost his balance, wobbling sideways.

Neil reached out, searching for something to hold as the floor disintegrated beneath him.

CHAPTER
SIXTY-TWO

"NEIL!" BREE SCREAMED.

Dangling on the edge of a new precipice, Neil grasped a piece of solid planking. He glanced up to find his sister perched safely on the edge of the broken windowsill. On his right, a few feet away, Andy clung to splintered remnants of the ballroom floor. The iron poker slipped out of his grasp and tumbled into the darkness below, landing after several seconds with a splash in the flooded basement.

It was a long drop. *Deadly*, Neil thought. Dust swirled all around, and as Neil found his breath, he began to choke.

"Stay where you are," said Bree. "I'm coming to get you."

"D-don't move," Neil managed to say. "You'll fall too."

Andy clambered forward, struggling to pull himself from the cavity. But the floor shuddered again and he lost his grip.

"Okay," said Bree. "Just . . . go slowly. Come toward me. Take my hand."

Neil tried, but as he released his left hand, he felt himself slipping. "I can't!" he said.

Bree glanced up. In shock, she stared over his shoulder toward the spot where Andy was struggling. Neil swiveled carefully and saw what had captured her attention. For a moment, he forgot where he was. He forgot everything.

Rebecca had returned. This time, she was no mere glimmer. She stood on the broken floor in front of her stepfather, dressed in her dirty hospital gown. Dirt caked her feet and ankles. Her dark hair hung like lake weed, draping her shoulders. Her face looked as it had in her final yearbook picture: empty, angry.

But she was no longer helpless. And she knew it. "Daddy . . ." Her voice was here now. It filled the room.

Andy froze. "Honey," he responded, as if she were as alive as an apple tree in autumn. "Please. Help me." He reached out for her, but she looked away.

Rebecca saw Neil. She saw Bree. She stared, but she did not acknowledge them. Neil's hope that she might help him was dashed when she turned back toward her stepfather and raised one foot over his head. Neil didn't have time to scream before she brought her heel down hard on the floor.

The wood collapsed with an ear-splitting blast. Andy screeched and slipped away into the shadows.

Neil's head rang and he struggled to maintain his grip as his fingers slid from the wet board.

At the windowsill, Bree reached for him, her eyes filled with panic. "Hurry!" she said. Neil reached out for her, but the planking he clung to gave a final squeal and pulled away from the wall. As he fell, the last thing Neil heard was his sister's horrified scream. Her face shrunk into nothingness, a pinpoint of terror before it disappeared altogether.

From below came a painful jolt.

Then a cold and serene darkness embraced him.

CHAPTER
SIXTY-THREE

HUDDLED ON THE WINDOWSILL, Bree clutched at the frame as the floor disappeared, taking her brother with it. She screamed so loud, her eyes teared up. The building shook with a terrible violence, as if it were releasing years of unspent rage at having been left alone out here in these woods. Bree briefly imagined the walls crumbling, the ceiling tumbling, the possibility of her own body crushed in the coming rubble.

She didn't care about any of that. All that mattered right now was saving Neil.

Bree turned away from the cloud of dust that had risen from the destruction and swung her legs over the jagged windowsill. Looking down, she knew the grass below was dangerously far away, but she didn't hesitate. As she slid forward, an excruciating pain bloomed as the window's broken glass cut through her jeans.

Then she was falling. The earth rose up quickly to meet her; she managed to roll into it. The soft ground broke her fall.

Ignoring the pain and the damp sensation in her hamstrings, she stood and kicked out a window adjacent to the one that had been boarded up. Neil was in there somewhere. She called his name, but received no answer. Hesitating only briefly, she leapt inside, splashing into the detritus, twisting her ankle by landing partially on a long wood plank.

The water shocked her. Her body buzzed with fear and hurt. When she tried to find the floor with her feet, she realized that she was nearly chest deep. She called Neil's name again.

Pieces of the ceiling continued to rain down, some close enough to splatter her face with wet particles of plaster and splinters of wood. With no small effort, she pushed through chunks of debris that bobbed on the water's surface.

As she searched, Bree imagined Andy's cold hook clutching her ankle and pulling her under. She began to panic, her lungs tight, her vision slanted.

Then, miraculously it seemed, she came upon Neil's body. Impossibly, he was sprawled out facedown on top of a table that was floating below one of the basketball hoops. His clothes were soaked, his hair a wet and matted mess. All thought left her but two words: *THANK GOD.*

She touched his face. It was surprisingly warm. Though he was unconscious, his breath greeted the palm of her hand like a small blessing. Glancing up, she noticed the jagged hole through which he'd fallen.

Deep inside a dark part of her mind, Bree knew that something had saved him — pulled him upon the table's surface — but she wouldn't allow herself to imagine who or what it had been. All she knew was that they needed to get out of there, before the rest of the building came tumbling down.

Holding on to the platform that held Neil's body aloft, Bree maneuvered several fallen boards against the wall, making a ramp upon which she dragged her brother out of the flood. Halfway to the window, the wood groaned beneath their weight. Bree scrambled faster, remembering a science-class lesson about how adrenaline gave people strength they couldn't usually access. Grasping his forearms, she managed to drag Neil up and over the threshold.

Outside, just as she inhaled a gasp of damp night air, she turned and saw something that took that breath away: an arm sticking out from underneath a heavy support beam. The rest of the body was facedown in the water.

Andrew Curtain was not moving. Bree shuddered as she realized with certainty that he'd never move again. For a moment, a wave of guilt crashed down upon her. This was not what she'd meant to happen. But then she looked down at Neil and the guilt gave way to anger.

She clutched her brother's limp body and pulled him farther from the building, embracing him, trying to warm him up. Shivering, she rubbed at his arms, his chest, trying to awaken whatever spark of life he had left inside him. "Please, please," she said to anyone who might be listening.

Seconds later, Neil opened his eyes and saw his sister's face. They both burst into tears.

CHAPTER
SIXTY-FOUR

A FEW DAYS LATER, the revelations of Andy's crimes whipped through Hedston and the surrounding area.

Some people believed that there had always been something strange about the man — an empty look in his eye, the fact that he continued to live alone so far out in the woods. Others refused to accept that he'd been capable of hurting anyone at all — to them, he was still Andy, good friend and kind neighbor.

At the pie shop, everyone had an opinion. As strange as their niece and nephew's story was, the aunts were certain that they were telling the truth, or at least most of it. What was most important to them, of course, was that Neil and Bree — who'd been scratched up and severely bruised — recover at their home as quickly as possible.

The police opened an investigation, discovering blood evidence near the fireplace in the Curtains' den, exactly where Neil and Bree had said it would be. The state was able to tie the DNA sample to Alice, corroborating their story.

When the local news covered the story, Neil and Bree were able to keep the promise they'd made to Mrs. Reilly — the one about revealing the truth of Nurse Janet's legacy. Not long afterward, her son, Nicholas, called the pie shop to apologize for harassing them. Claire and Anna had no idea who he was or what he was talking about.

Even though the specter of Nurse Janet was finally laid to rest, there was a new tale for the children of Hedston to share in the dead of night: the Legend of Rebecca Smith, the Ghost of Graylock, who, with a little help from the living, had managed to avenge her own murder from beyond the grave.

Several months after returning to New Jersey, Neil was keeping in touch with Wesley, chatting online and on the phone every now and again. To Neil's surprise, he'd overheard Bree talking with Eric a few times, mostly about music and new bands they thought each other might like.

His mother, Linda, continued to see her doctors. At home, Neil was happy to find her beginning to act like herself again — mostly, as Linda explained, because she realized that she was actually better off without Rick, who'd taken the hint and rented an apartment in Manhattan where he could keep trying to live out that dream of his. He even had a spare room for when his kids came to visit.

His family was changing. It wasn't easy. It never would be. But Neil understood that it was for the best.

One night in late October, while Neil, Bree, and Linda were eating dinner together, the phone rang. Neil answered. A woman introduced herself and explained that she was a producer for a television program called *Ghostly Investigators*. Neil nearly dropped the receiver.

"Hello? Mr. Cady? Are you there?"

"I, uh, I'm here," Neil stammered. His mother and sister watched from the kitchen table. "No one's ever called me Mr. Cady before."

"Okay, Neil. Well, Alexi and Mark heard about your experience up in Hedston. They want to do a show about Graylock Hall. Would you and your sister be interested in speaking to them?"

Epilogue

NEIL WAS RUNNING THROUGH THE DARKNESS. Lightning flashed, illuminating a hateful sky and furious whitecaps out in the middle of the lake. Wind whipped his hair away from his face as thunder struck, sending his heart into a frenzy. He glanced over his shoulder and saw the flashlight in the distance behind him growing ever closer.

The only way out was through the reeds at the water's edge. He knew what would happen if he went that way. But what choice did he have? He was barefoot and bleeding. And the man was nearly at his heels.

Neil stumbled into the shallows and immediately fell forward. The reeds bent and caught him, and he managed to find his footing before landing on his face. Over his shoulder, the bobbing light was closer. He heard the fall of heavy boots approaching.

Just get out past the weeds, he told himself. *The open water will be safe. He can't reach you there.*

Neil pushed forward only to find the slimy stalks wrapping around his ankles again. This always happened — the nightmare was always the same. So why didn't he learn?

"REBECCA . . ." The voice bellowed in the space directly behind him.

I'm not Rebecca, Neil wanted to call out. But a blow to his shoulder knocked him down. He sunk below the water. It filled his nose and mouth, and he choked.

Fuzzy strands of lake weed caught his wrists. The more he struggled, the tighter they became. He tried to spin, to see the face of the man who'd been chasing him, but the flashlight struck the water's surface from above, obscuring what was behind it.

His clenched lungs grew weary, exhausted. *Let it go,* he thought. *Give up. Drown. It's what happened to her. It's what always happens.*

Neil hadn't dreamed about Rebecca Smith in a long time. Images of her death had disappeared from his imagination several months ago. Now that he was back in Hedston, the memories had returned.

The chase had been only one of many dreams in which she'd haunted him. The worst was the dream in which he clung to the edge of the broken floor in Graylock's ballroom. Rebecca stood over him, glaring at him as she raised her foot and brought it down. He'd always wake with a start, the same question running through his head.

Why, Rebecca? Why?

He'd done as she'd asked — followed her glowing bread crumbs along the twisted trail. And his reward had been her betrayal.

Why?

Maybe she'd been blinded by her hatred of Andy, by her need for revenge. Maybe she'd wanted to give up, but something in her nature, or Nature itself, hadn't allowed it. Neil was familiar with this problem. His mother had recently told him: *We ask our brain to stop worrying, stop obsessing, stop dreaming the same scary dreams again and again. But our brains rarely take requests.*

He'd become resigned to the idea that he'd never know why Rebecca had done what she'd done. And so the dreams had come, presenting the question again and again. He wondered if Rebecca was sending them to him. But he also took comfort in knowing that sometimes dreams are just dreams.

In the water, in the dream, he yanked his wrists up and around. The light from above grew brighter as the weeds tightened even more. His fingertips began to feel numb. The cold seeped into his skin, injecting him with a chill he felt he'd never escape. His chest began to ache as his lungs begged for air. His skin cried out as those familiar pins and needles stuck him over and over.

This wasn't supposed to happen. This felt real, not dreamlike at all. He opened his mouth to scream for help, but all that sounded was a pathetic cry muffled by bubbles.

If he didn't get air soon, he'd die. He knew this was true.

With eyes open wide, he glanced around in the darkness for something to use to cut himself loose. There was nothing except emptiness and water and the beyond.

Then a pale face appeared several yards away. As it came closer, he struggled even more. Rebecca's blue eyes looked into his own. Her dark hair swirled around her face, lifted by invisible currents. Her mouth was pulled back in an amused and terrible smile. As she reached out for him, Neil screamed again.

But then she touched him. Her fingers encompassed his captured wrists, and Neil felt a strange quiet. The smile she wore wasn't terrible after all. Had it ever been?

"*Be still*," she said. Her voice was sweet, echoing in the dark water as it would down a long hallway.

Neil stopped moving and watched in amazement as the weeds

loosened, then fell away. The cold abated, and he found he no longer needed to draw air. He felt no pain. He hovered in the darkness with Rebecca — the girl he'd come to fear more than anything in his life, which was saying a lot. She stared at him as if in wonder, her mouth open as if she wanted to speak but couldn't.

He knew he had something to ask her, but his mind had gone blank.

He looked into her eyes, and the word came.

"Why?"

Rebecca's face drew in on itself — a look of profound shame. If she'd been capable of spilling tears, Neil understood that she would have filled the lake with salt water.

"I'm sorry," she said. *"Forgive me."*

Was this enough? After everything she'd put him through? He thought of his mother, of how difficult it had been for her to come so far, and she'd had help. Rebecca had been alone for such a long time before she'd found someone who might understand. She'd chosen him. And he'd chosen to listen.

Was this enough? Probably not. But if he were to listen to her now, he would need to make another choice. To forgive.

Surprising himself, he nodded slightly. Rebecca's mouth curled into a sad smile.

They stayed that way for several more moments, holding hands in the darkness. Then Rebecca glanced toward the surface. When Neil looked up, he noticed that the light from above appeared to have changed. Instead of bobbing like a flashlight beam, the illumination cast a diffuse glow that fell through the water like the moon's silver gaze.

She looked once more into his eyes and said, "*Thank you, Neil.*" She released his hands and kicked for the surface.

Quickly, he realized there was no surface. They were floating in a darkness deeper than the one at Graylock Lake. And he knew that the light was farther away than the moon was from the Earth.

Rebecca appeared to grow small as she ascended into an illusion of distance. When both she and the mysterious silver light had finally gone, Neil woke up.

All was dark, and for a moment he had a difficult time distinguishing this room. But soon, his eyes made out the bedposts near his feet. He was at the aunts' house. It was November; the night before he and Bree and Eric and Wesley went back to Graylock Island, to film the interview with *Ghostly Investigators*.

Neil sat up, filled with a discomforting, unnameable emotion.

Someone sat on the end of his bed, a hunched shadow, long hair falling past her shoulders, hiding her face. Neil gasped. The figure reached out and touched his leg. "It's just me."

"Bree?"

"Who else?"

Rebecca's face flashed through his mind. Neil felt for his sister's hand. "I just had the strangest dream," he said.

Bree sniffed. "Why do you think I'm here?"

Neil bit his lip. "She came to you too?" Even in the darkness, he saw her nod. He considered what this meant. So many things.

"She apologized," Bree said.

"Why did she wait so long?"

"I don't know. Maybe she needed us close by. In Hedston."

"Yeah. Or maybe she was scared what we'd say if she tried." How odd it was to think of a ghost being scared. He supposed he had Bree to thank for that.

"Either way, I don't think she'll be visiting us again," said Bree.

Neil had imagined that hearing those words come from his sister's mouth would have filled him with a sense of joy. But they didn't.

"Shove over," said Bree, laying down on top of the covers. Neil made room. Together, they stared silently at the dark ceiling for a long while, listening to the creaking, cracking sounds that came naturally at night in an old house.

By the time the pale dawn light began to filter through the bedroom's gauzy curtains, Neil had stumbled upon a deep and welcome sleep in which his dreams were finally his own.

ACKNOWLEDGMENTS

To my friends and family, who are always so supportive while I write these crazy things.

To Nick Eliopulos, my supereditor; and to David Levithan and the awesome team at Scholastic for making this book happen.

To Barry Goldblatt for kicking all the necessary butt.

To Libba Bray, Robin Wasserman, Colleen A.F. Venable, and Barry Lyga for commiserating at cafés.

To Shane Rebenschied for the glorious cover illustration and to Christopher Stengel for the beautiful design.

To Richard Hawkins and Sharon Hird for all they do.

And finally, to everyone who's sent kind letters and e-mails about my books . . .

Thank you, thank you, thank you!